# SEVENTH JOURNEY

# SEVENTH JOURNEY

## BOOK 2

ROBERT J. R. GRAHAM

# SEVENTH JOURNEY
## BOOK II

iUniverse books may be ordered through booksellers or by contacting:

iUniverse
1663 Liberty Drive
Bloomington, IN 47403
www.iuniverse.com
1-800-Authors (1-800-288-4677)

ISBN: 978-1-4917-5376-7 (sc)
ISBN: 978-1-4917-5377-4 (e)

Library of Congress Control Number: 2014922477

Printed in the United States of America.

iUniverse rev. date: 01/14/2015

# CONTENTS

# ETHER

# PROLOGUE

George was part of one of those fortunate northern villages yet untouched by the darkness, so he was shocked when he found a mysterious man lying in a crater, deep in the snow. The crater was perfectly round, and George could still remember the sound of the steam rising from it. The hole was mysteriously warm amidst a bitter cold -21 winter day. Venturing closer, George peered into the crater and realized the man was still alive. He lay there, naked. The heat from the crater began to wear off and the cold started to set in. George quickly wrapped the man up with his coat and gave him a cup of tea in a thermos he carried with him. The man shivered and drank from the metal cup.

"Who are you? Are you okay?" George asked. The man remained silent, shivering violently.

"Listen to me, are you hurt? Do you understand what I'm saying?" The man looked up at George as if to say that he did, but the words wouldn't come out.

"Can you understand me? Nod your head if you do." The man slowly nodded his head.

"Okay good. Are you hurt?" The man shook his head.

"How did you get here? Do you know what happened to you?" He sat in silence. George paused for a moment, and then helped the man to his feet.

"You're coming with me. Let's go. You can't stay here." The man got up and hobbled alongside George back to his vehicle. He looked as though he was in his thirties.

"Listen to me, son, you're fine now. I'm going to take you back to my house. Do you have a name?"

"I don't know, I can't remember." The man finally spoke.

"Do you remember anything?" The man shook his head.

"All right then, for now I'm calling you James. It was a good friend's name. Let's hope you turn out to be a good friend too." He gave James some spare clothes from his truck. George began driving back to the house, and thought that whatever had happened to James must be from another world. Possibly even alien. The crater he was laying in wasn't man made, and even if it was, there wasn't a soul around for kilometres. The way it steamed reminded him of an old story his people would tell, one of the few stories they had about ancient times. It spoke of visitors coming down from the sky that burned into the ground and left impressions in the earth. But that was only a story.

"James, what else can you tell me? Talk to me."

James looked around. "We're exactly 300 feet above sea level. The barometric pressure is 38 percent."

"My God, son, how do you know that?" George stared at him in shock.

"It's on your dashboard," James replied with a hint of a smile.

"Well, at least you can read. Anything else you'd like to tell me?"

"All I remember is a flash, a really bright light, but then I had the wind knocked out of out of me. I must have slammed into the ground, 'cause the next thing I remember was you waking me up. Thank you for the tea."

"You're welcome, James. Well just mind yourself from now on and we're going to get along just fine."

"Mind myself?" James looked at him inquisitively.

"What are you, some kind of idiot?"

"No, I'm not an idiot. I just don't remember anything. But I'm looking around and I know things."

"Like what?"

"I know those mountains outside are 25,092 feet high. I know exactly how cold it is. I know what kind of truck this is, how many cylinders it has, and how to perform basic repairs on it. I'm pretty sure I know how to drive stick shift also. I'm seeing machines out in the fields, and I know how to use them. Things are coming to me slowly." James stared out the window as he spoke before slowly looking back at George.

"Well, let's just give it some time. Why don't you relax now and maybe your memory will come back on its own. We'll be home in a bit, and you can meet Jessica. In time, you'll get better, I'm sure." George spoke sympathetically.

James smiled at him. "Thank you. You're a very kind man."

"I'd hope someone would do the same for me, if I ever fell out of the sky."

"Is that what you think happened to me?" James looked at George.

"I don't really see any other explanation. There was no one out there for miles around you. No car, no boat, and no clothes. The crater you were in was round, like from an impact. And it was hot. Steaming, actually."

James noticed George squirm uncomfortably.

"I don't know. Yeah, maybe you're right, I mean how else could I have gotten here?" James nodded slowly, processing the information.

"I'm not sure either, James. Maybe your memory will come back and you'll be able to tell us more."

"I hope so." James nodded again and sighed. "Why are you so accepting of me, George? You've been extremely generous." James wrapped himself tighter in a blanket on the front seat, still recovering from the cold.

"What would you rather I do? Leave you to freeze to death out there? If you're not up to staying with me, you can certainly try to find another place in town. But without any clothes or money, that might be hard."

"I'm sorry, I meant no disrespect. I am just not used to such generosity, I guess. You were right, though; my memory seems to come back when I look at certain things. Like when I look outside, I see water towers, and I immediately understand what they are for. And I understand many of the inner workings of things I'm looking at, as if I can peer directly into the essential nature of the object. But my memories or anything personal about me seems to be lost."

"That's interesting. Do you know what a hamburger is?"

"Of course."

"Good. We're almost home. Are you hungry? You must be hungry." George pulled into a diner off the interstate. The sign above the door read Joey's Fish & Chips. The diner was just off I-95, and a good place to stop for a bite to eat.

"Do you remember your last meal?" George asked as they both climbed out of the truck and walked towards the door.

"No, I don't. This would be a first for me." James sighed as he followed George into the diner.

"I doubt that, or how else could you be alive if you haven't eaten until now? Have a seat at a booth; I'll be there in a minute." George made his way to the restroom, motioning for a nearby waitress to get a couple of coffees for them. James sat down, taking in as much of his surroundings as he could. James sat there quietly until the waitress came by with the coffee.

"Here you go. Would you like anything else, hon?" The waitress smiled at him.

"Like what?" He looked up at her, confused.

"We have a bacon and eggs breakfast special on the menu, do you want that?"

"Sure, I'll get one of those."

"Comin' up." The waitress walked away just as George sat back down.

"I'm getting the bacon and eggs breakfast special."

"Nice choice. Did you order me one?"

"No I..." James stuttered and looked at George with some alarm.

"Excuse me; I'll have a breakfast special too!" George shouted at the waitress, who acknowledged the additional order with a nod.

"Just so you know, the regular etiquette is that folks eat together."

"Etiquette?" James tilted his head as he looked at George.

"Yes, it's just the way we do things around here. We're a big family. You'll get the hang of it." George smiled and patted James on the shoulder.

"I see." James nodded and looked out the window.

George finally had a moment to take a look at James. He was fit young man, in his early 30's with dark brown hair and white complexion. His eyes were blue, but they weren't normal. The blue shot out from the iris like a starburst, much like that of an old toy doll.

"So James, do you know where you're headed, or what you're doing?"

"I really don't, I'm sorry. For now, I'm just trying to figure things out. If you hadn't found me, I think I would be dead right now. I'm still recovering from that."

"Fair enough, you can have more time to figure things out while you're at my place. As long as you respect me and my daughter, and help out when I need you, you are welcome to stay as long as you need."

"Sure, that won't be a problem at all, George; I already have tremendous respect for you. I won't be a problem for you."

"I know you won't. I've got a good feeling about you. Let's enjoy some breakfast." George said as the waitress appeared with both their orders. The two of them sat and ate their breakfast awhile longer before heading to George's place.

James looked out the window and observed the frigid weather taking its toll on the village around him. The people were used to it, though: everyone dressed for the weather, except him apparently.

James considered George's hospitality as they drove along. He would stay only a while with him, at least until he got his memory back. There were familiar things around George's house; James would occasionally stumble across an item that reminded him of a time long ago. A life of science and research, so unfamiliar to him now, yet somehow these memories lingered. He met Jessica, George's daughter. She was a young teenager, full of energy and curiosity. She bombarded James with questions, most of which he couldn't answer. If only he could remember his past, James thought to himself.

"Jessica, since you like to make a game out of asking me about my past, I have a question for you. Do you remember everything from when you were young?" James asked while sitting in George's cozy living room.

"No, not everything. Mostly the good things and some scary things," Jessica said, looking over at him.

"Scary things?"

"Yeah, there was a time when I could see things that weren't there. At least, that's what I thought."

"Were you dreaming?"

"No, these things happened when I was awake." Jessica sat back in her favourite arm chair. It was green, and old with a ridiculous pattern on it, but it's where her mom used to read to her.

"What do you mean they weren't there?"

"I saw them. As clearly as I see you now. Pictures moved, so did statues. I saw creatures roaming around that no one else could see."

"What kind of creatures?"

"I don't know, like little gremlins. I know it sounds crazy."

"I'm listening."

"I would stare at the edge of my bed, and I'd see small gremlins or trolls pop up and talk to each other. I would see toys or statues move, and things that didn't make sense. But it was really real to me," Jessica said as she shifted in her seat and stared aimlessly over James's head.

"What did your father think?"

"In our culture, people that see things that others cannot are considered a gateway. And that meant a life of training with our spirit teacher and we didn't want to go through that. It's better than being called schizophrenic, which is what the doctor told me. Like I said, everyone thought I was crazy."

"So what happened, did it just stop?"

"It stopped, yes. One day it got so real that I was afraid for my sanity, and begged God to take it away. I cried myself to sleep. After I woke up, it stopped."

"I see."

"You must think I'm crazy. I'll shut up now."

"No, please continue."

"Once, I was about to go to sleep, when one of the trolls at the edge of my bed popped up, and said there was a demon in the house, and that I had to wake up. He said the demon takes souls that are sleeping. Over the fireplace in my grandparents' house was an old toy soldier. It was a wooden, hand-carved piece. It jumped off the wall and walked right past my room into my grandfather's room." She shivered.

"Then what happened?" James leaned forward, waiting for Jessica to continue.

"My mom woke me up later that night, crying because my grandfather had had a heart attack and died. I knew it had to have been the soldier. What do you think, James?" Jessica looked at him with sad, haunted eyes.

"It's possible, yes." James spoke honestly.

"Really? You don't think I'm joking? No one ever believes me when I tell them that."

"I think there's a lot we don't understand, and too much that we just don't want to think about. If it were real, we'd have to rethink many things about our world. So yes, I think your story is possible, and it was certainly real to you."

"Thank you, but why doesn't anyone else believe me?" Jessica looked sad once more.

"It's easier to ignore things sometimes. That's the way most people go about life, and it's a slow process to make them change." James stood up from the living room couch, admiring some ancient hand carved masks.

"Yes, I guess you're right. It's either that, or I'm crazy." Jessica relaxed and leaned back in her seat.

"You're not crazy. What you saw was real, and it happened—for you. If no one else was receptive, that doesn't mean it's your fault. You just saw more than others are willing to see." James turned to look at her.

"Thanks James, you've made me feel a lot better. Other experiences like that have been happening to me my entire life."

"Yes, I imagine they would. I can't remember any of my own experiences, or else I'd share—but I certainly believe it's all possible." James shrugged and turned back to admire the art.

"Thanks for listening either way." Jessica smiled at him and stood up.

"No problem. Maybe you can help me too. Do you know anything about a corporation called Netex? I have been having dreams lately, and this company keeps coming up."

"That's one of the worst companies in the world. I mean, they caused all of this."

"All of what? What did they do?"

"George said I shouldn't talk about this stuff, that they're listening to us and if I talk about it…"

"Who is listening? What did they do?"

"No I can't James."

"You have to talk to me, please. Maybe it'll help me remember my past. If you know something, I need to know."

"All I know is that it's where the monsters came from. They invented things, and it went too far. They created weapons, and lots of people died. Cities are gone now, there's so much war."

"Do you know what they invented?"

"They made something that mutated people, and poisoned them. The water went bad, and there was chaos in the streets."

"Was there any army left? Did they try to stop Netex?"

"It was too late. Please James, I don't feel right talking about this."

"I'm sorry. Thank you for letting me stay here Jessica. I know it's not easy to have a new person around. I don't always understand your culture, and so much of my own past is a mystery."

"It's okay. Somehow I feel safer with you here, but if you want to know more you should talk to George."

She walked back to her room, as James went out and helped George fortify the cabin with extra wood from the shed. An ice storm was coming, and they weren't sure how the old house would handle it.

# PART I

## MATTER

*"As Jacob, you were brilliant and actually invented a technology which bridged the gap between dimensions. You used this technology to tap in and shift into different perspectives and dimensions of experience. This technology was far beyond anything created on your planet for thousands of years."*

# ONE

## STORMS COMING

L IFE HAS A beginning, an adventure, and an ending. On an ordinary day, James woke up with that thought lingering in his mind, and a pain that wouldn't go away. He lifted himself up off the bed, put on his heavy coat, and walked out towards the precipice overlooking the ice-covered mountains surrounding them.

He sat down and looked out over the hills of ice as snow drifts blew in the whistling wind. The sun washed over the sky with a reddish orange glow that seemed so familiar to him, almost as if the heavens had opened up. He barely noticed the cold; it was far too pleasant a morning to allow that to distract him.

Time raced by him as he sat there, wondering about the strangeness of his circumstances, and of his memory loss.

The snow coated the needles of the surrounding pine trees, white upon green. These trees, these lungs of the earth were scattered upon hilltops for miles and miles. James looked over his shoulder, and saw his adopted family walking towards him over the hillside.

George willingly accepted James into his life, without knowing anything about him, and even in spite of his memory loss. They were his family now. How could they be so kind in a world so distraught and in pain? How strange it was that they extended their generosity towards a man without even a name. James often pondered these things, but came to accept that he might never know.

"James!"

Jessica hiked up the trail towards him, lifting up her homemade maroon dress as she went. Her long brown hair bounced as she climbed steadily upward. She was in her early teens, innocent and smart. She had similar features to George, just younger and feminine. She didn't look like her mother from what James could tell from pictures. She had dark black hair, a reddish brown complexion, and bright brown eyes. At times it seemed like she saw much more than she led everyone to believe.

"What's the rush, Jess?"

"Dad needs your help. He wants you to go talk to him. He's out by the back of the house. He said it was an emergency!" She said, trying to catch her breath.

"Okay I'll be right there." They lived close to Ungava Bay, a frozen ice land with an unforgiving and relentless winter that constantly pounded the town with mountains of snow. The rolling hills gave way to the trees and, of course, the often frozen water around the local valleys. Their house was just a few hundred yards away from the rest of the town. It was a modest village; they were a fishing and hunting people that forged their way through the constant cold to survive.

The house itself was a unique back split, designed by George, with the back of the house and the basement actually built under water. If someone went into the house and towards the basement they would see reinforced windows that acted as submarine portals looking out into the bay. James saw fish from time to time, but mostly deep blue waters that mesmerized him for hours. If George was out back, he'd be by the immersion shafts that supported the underwater portion of the house. James made his way through the snow to meet George.

"Hey, Jess said you needed me." George was an older man, perhaps in his late 50's, with lines of wisdom throughout his strong but worn face. He wore a grey parka and black fishing boots, his normal work attire. He was the one who found James naked in a steaming crater. When George woke him, he was the first thing James saw, and without him he would have surely died out there.

"James, for weeks now, the temperature has been dropping too fast, and it's causing a buildup of ice. The extra weight on the back of the house is putting strain on the supports. We need the ice chipper by the quarry to grind away the ice surrounding the house and then reinforce it with the wood from last season. If we don't do that tonight, the basement might crack open."

"Really?" James looked at George in alarm.

"Yes. The weight of this new ice will cause the house to slide backwards, shattering the glass in the basement, and causing the water to pour in. The house will be destroyed. We need to fix it now. I don't know why there is extra ice this season, but it's been getting worse every year."

"Does it have anything to do with the madness in the cities?" Jess asked.

"No. Don't talk about such things." George said sharply as he turned away from her. George never spoke of what he saw during his last trip into the city. "We need to get the ice chipper right now; otherwise the house may not last the next few hours."

"Okay, I'll go start the truck."

"We need gas first; the quarry is far away." As they were talking, Jess approached them.

"Are you going to the quarry? I want to go with you!"

"No. The quarry is no place for a young girl." George said firmly

"Dad, I want to come with you! Please let me come and see all the ice walls at the quarry. I want to go to the store too!"

"Okay, Jessica, you can come, but you have to stay in the car at the quarry. I don't want you walking around with all the machinery nearby."

"Thanks, Dad. I love you!"

"Humph. Go get ready, we have to leave soon." Jessica ran off to get changed.

James was fine with helping, but couldn't resist asking about his circumstances one more time.

"George, let me ask you something, the day you found me, can you tell me again what happened?"

"James, I've told you this story several times, and there is nothing more to say."

"There must be something, some detail there that I'm missing, something that might link me to my past."

"Why do you want to be connected with your past? There is an Inuit proverb that my people believe in: "Yesterday is ashes; tomorrow wood. Only today the fire shines brightly. The past is not important; it is who you are, and what you do now that matters. Tomorrow hasn't happened yet, and we have only now to live our lives. Live it to the best of your ability, and look towards the future."

"I understand, but you have people, you have a history. You have proverbs to speak of, wisdom to share from experience and culture. I have none of those things."

"You have people now. Never forget that. We are your people."

"Please, George, one last time." He looked at James, showing his annoyance. But James needed to know; it was eating away at him.

"When I walked north of the Great Bay, I found a fishing hole where the ice was broken. It seemed as though someone was there, someone not of this place. If the ice was broken by my people for fishing, it would have been done with more care. This seemed like something else. It was deliberate, and violent. I looked around for tracks, but there was nothing close by. As I looked around, out of the corner of my eye, I saw a flash over the hills. I continued towards the light, and once I reached the top, I saw you at the bottom on the other side. You were nearly frozen to death; you looked red and blue, nearly frost-bitten in your hands and feet. You were in some sort of crater, finely pressed snow surrounded you. It was a perfect circle you were lying in. I ran down to you, and you were still breathing. You couldn't have been there for very long, otherwise you would have been dead. There were no tracks, clothes or possessions. You were naked and left for dead. That's all."

"What do you think the light was? Was it just the sun reflecting off of the hill tops or was it something more?"

"It was something else. The earth moved."

"Moved?" He looked at George in confusion.

"There was a rumbling, a vibration in the earth that happened at the same time as the flash. It was not natural."

"And there was nothing around me? No clothes, no tracks…" James trailed off, hopeful for more.

"Nothing. Beyond those hills is just endless snow. There was nowhere you could have come from and nowhere for you to go. Just frozen death and us. I took it as a sign that we were meant to bring you home."

"Is that why you saved me?"

"Yes, but also because you are human, and you have as much right to live as any man does. It is not my place to deprive people of life, but to help those who need it. If I had been able to help you yet did nothing, then I would have been implicated in your death. I couldn't have that weight on my shoulders. In my tribe, James, we give of ourselves freely and take only that which is needed. You needed help, and I only acted naturally."

"Thank you. You are a good man." James squeezed his shoulder and gave him a grateful smile.

"We have another saying in my tribe, James: 'You never really know your friends from your enemies until the ice breaks.'"

"I see."

"When the ice breaks, James, I will be there for you. You have been helpful to me and Jessica; you have been of great assistance during the hunt. You helped cut wood and helped me maintain our home. You have been a blessing, James, and I am getting old. I cannot protect Jessica forever, especially not from what lies south of here."

"What is south? Why won't you tell me?"

"I have spoken to our elders, and they have asked me not to discuss it with you. In time, you will discover what lies south of us. For now, be satisfied with your life, and help me remove this ice. We don't have much time."

"Of course, let's move."

James walked towards George's old red pickup parked just in front of the house. He wasn't sure how he remembered how to drive, but the skill was there when he needed it, along with many other abilities.

The truck was quite old, by 20 years at least. It ran and the heater worked, and that's all that mattered. James got in and waited for Jessica and George. They soon followed and they drove towards the quarry. He knew the owner quite well and, when they needed extra money, George would work for him. James would help sometimes as well, but he would usually be sent on errands instead. The ice quarry had several large ice-breaking trucks with mechanical arms and thrashing rollers mounted in front. These were often used to cut through ice and snow to make new roads.

They got in and we drove towards the gas station, about 20 kilometres up the road. George had brought the money and some extra canisters to fill up. It was a quiet drive, the silence only broken by a few observations made by Jess. She loved the snow, and was amazed by the size of the ice walls along the side of the road.

When they arrived at the gas station, James had a bad feeling. Something wasn't right. He got out of the truck and began to fill up while Jess waited in the car and George went in to pay. Parked adjacent to them was a group of men that were eating near the Chip and Burger truck. They were bikers and very rough looking. They weren't local. There were eight of them and they seemed to be eyeing Jessica and James.

James knew there were some unsavoury characters that showed up here because it was the only gas station for 50 kilometres in any direction. If you needed gas, you were coming here. They noticed George take out his wallet on his way inside, and they kept looking at their truck, which James caught out of the corner of his eye. His senses were heightened at the possibility of conflict.

They looked at each other, with a few of them talking to the rest. They began to pick up their things, made their way back to the bikes, and drove off up the street. The only street, in fact, that connected Jessica, James, and George with the quarry. After paying, George came back with some chocolates for Jessica. She was happy, but James was cautious. The gang of men had gone up the road ahead of them, so James drove slowly up the street to give them some distance, but it didn't matter. They had driven about two kilometres when they came across the men blocking off the road, waiting for them.

"What do they want?" Jess had obviously not picked up on their dominant posture. There was no question that they meant harm. Their laughter reminded James of a time long ago, an emotion, and a familiarity with their brutish glares. He knew what they wanted, and they couldn't have it.

"They are hostile, James; we should go back to the gas station. We can call the police." George had the right idea, but the problem was, these men would follow.

"No, this has to be dealt with now. I'm getting out."

"James, no! Stay in the truck with us, let's just turn around. It's safer." Jess said. It was evident from her clenched fists that she was frightened.

"No, it has to be this way, otherwise they won't stop." He opened the door.

"It's not worth it, let's turn around now," George pleaded. James looked back at George, who saw his eyes. James saw George's own eyes widen as he reluctantly nodded. James got out of the truck, closed the door and walked towards them.

"Hi there. We'd like to get by, so please move aside so that we can pass." A few of the men burst out laughing; others smiled and shook their heads. The rest proceed to get things out of their cars. This wasn't going to be pretty.

"Ah, you want to pass, do you? This is our highway. You need to pay the toll."

"What's your toll?" James asked calmly.

"Hmm, give us all of your money and the girl too." As they moved closer to him, James dug into some form of stance. As he did, a flood of memories—no, abilities—overtook him. There was a part of him that was about to be unleashed. It felt automatic.

"Not a chance," he said.

"Well it looks like we'll have to do this the fun way." If this guy was their leader, he wasn't impressive. He was thin and scrawny, wearing a leather jacket and blue jeans. He had greasy, black curly hair and soulless black eyes. He had a face that reminded James of a hawk.

They walked towards him, five of them directly surrounding James, with six or seven more waiting in their cars. James's combative abilities held together, as he mentally prepared himself. He didn't know where this understanding of the combative process came from, but he was able to observe their every move and quickly perceive their combative potential, with an immediate knowledge of which techniques and strategies he would utilize to deal with them. He was able to calculate the distance between himself and his opponents with great ease. There was no fear in his heart as he stepped towards the pack of unruly men.

Their leader called to James, "You've made a big mistake coming here. Now we have to kill you. Not only that, but we're going to kill that girl in the truck too." He smirked.

"Stop talking, and come kill me. I'm waiting," James said to them. If they were going to do something, they should get it over with. They were still out of distance but James moved to a formal fighting bow stance, and awaited their advancement. His classical form seemed to have stymied them for an instant. They shook off their confusion and closed the distance fast. James dug in his stance. The ground cracked beneath him, as he exerted a tremendous force grinding into the dirt.

James looked back at the truck for a brief second and saw that George was about to get out. "George, get back in the truck. Go back and get Jess out of here now. I'll deal with this."

He looked at James and nodded, getting back in the truck and closing the door as he started up the engine. James heard them pull away as he watched his opponents in front of him. He knew George was not willingly retreating, he was just getting Jessica out of there. He would not leave James to die, but he must protect her first and James understood that.

The largest brute of the group charged James in what seemed like slow motion. He stared at the man, observing his movements and taking in tremendous amounts of information about him. James awaited his trigger, the time to strike. *Not yet.* The man moved closer and closer. Time almost stood still as James observed the smallest micro-movements. He was approaching fast, yet it seemed like James had all the time in the world. The man was big, and sluggish. James prepared to yield as he closed in on his position.

James moved quickly to the left as the man charged forward with his head down. James moved only a half-step away to leave room for his strike to the man's head. James' hand connected with the man's temple and he fell to the ground, most likely dead.

The next man approached in haste and James yielded to strike his groin. He buckled over as James quickly grabbed his head and connected his knee to the man's nose, crushing it, and rendering him maimed and bleeding on the snow.

The next approached with caution, carrying an iron pipe of some sort. James coiled his body in a cat stance as the man lunged, swinging the pipe. He missed as James parried his arm out of the way from a close position, and struck the man's eyes. He was temporarily blind, and now screaming and curled up, bleeding all over the snow. *Next, James* thought.

He noticed some of those in the background get up while others began to grab weapons. Next was a flurry of blows to several combatants. As a mad rush occurred, James felt calm as he connected with multiple strikes. There were only a few left standing. They surrounded James quickly and began to charge at him. He lashed forward with a flurry of strikes, and the last of them went down.

The few that remained observed their fallen gang members lying in pools of their own blood with James alone standing amidst their bodies. They rushed backwards, almost tripping over themselves towards their cars. They got into their vehicles and took off up the road.

The scene around James brought back a fierce memory from a lifetime ago, where violence was all that made sense. There was something about the blood and bodies that brought it all back. James recalled a powerful adversary, guarded by several large men. He remembered engaging with them. They were physically challenging to deal with because they possessed super human strength. He tried to recall a name, a place, but all he could come up with was *Kane*. He saw himself toppling the smoke and shadow creature, but it was too late. He was already stabbed in the back by Kane, which ended the fight, and his life.

Yet after all that, there was a sense of peace and calm as the world burned around him. He remembered floating through a tunnel, but that was all. Now he was here.

The adrenaline left him as his body shook from the confrontation and the full gravity of the situation hit him. *I'm alive and they are not.* He stood up, and walked around, looking at the mess. He needed transportation.

# TWO

## INSIGHT

JAMES MADE HIS way back to the gas station, and found George and Jess waiting for him, as if they knew to wait for him, as if they knew James could handle it. George looked at James as he walked up the street, and gave him a solemn nod of respect and gratitude. He approached cautiously, as if he could still smell blood. "James, what happened back there? How did you—"

James cut him off. "I'm not sure how it happened, but they're gone now. That's all that counts."

"Yes. That's all that matters now." He regained his composure. "Since you've arrived, you've demonstrated many amazing abilities. You are a wizard with electronics and mechanical things; you know first aid; you know how to fish in our arctic sea, better than some of our natives. It's rare we've ever seen one with your ability to hunt. This is just the tip of the iceberg, and now, now you can fight, too?"

"I don't know if I can call it fighting It...it was something else altogether. I was prepared to kill them all, had they not left in time." James remembered how he had so easily and calmly dismantled them.

"I don't know what you did, but you made them go away. What happened?"

"It's not important now, we need to move; the house won't be able to support itself much longer. The ice storm was worse than we expected. The stilts are coming loose, and I need your help to put it back together. Let's go grab that ice crusher before it gets dark." George turned towards Jess. "Come on, honey! We need to go, now!"

Jess ran towards them. She had been wandering around, giving them time to talk.

A short while later they arrived home with the ice crusher, as Jess liked to call it. George called it that too, but it was essentially an oversized tractor, built to cut holes in the ice. They used it to cut their way through to the base of the stilts, allowing them to reinforce them using cement re-bar. It would hold, for now.

James went inside after working with George throughout the night. He lay down and instantly fell asleep.

There was a flash of brilliant white light, a dark tunnel and a doorway at the end of a seemingly never ending passageway. James willed himself to move closer, instantly feeling the cold of the darkness. A presence was all around him, something—or someone—was in the darkness. He could feel it and it wanted him.

The light beckoned toward him, making him feel warmth and acceptance, despite the chilling grasp of the darkness. He moved closer to the light, faster now. James looked towards the darkness and felt lost immediately. He was overwhelmed and isolated. His body began to feel tired, negative. Thoughts of despair entered his mind. *What was the point? Why not just let go and join the darkness? It doesn't matter, nobody loves me. Nobody knows me, I have no family, and I'm all alone in this world anyway. Why not step into the darkness? No one would care, would they?*

James shook off the desperation and turned back towards the light. The warmth surrounded him again, and all at once a feeling of completeness and wholeness rushed through his soul. He realized that oneness and unity was all there really was. *That* was real, not the darkness. James snapped back to reality, and quickly rushed through the portal and into the light.

He found himself standing upon an orange sand dune with a pure blue sky above. He looked towards the horizon to discern any signs of life and noticed a patch of white structure way off in the distance. Due to its size, James figured it must be some sort of village or city. He looked around in all directions, but nothing else could be seen from his vantage point.

He walked towards the city, noticing the sand as it avalanched down towards the base of the dune. He could not believe how real it all seemed. He felt the heat of the sun, wind, and sand. His vision was perfectly clear, his body light and supple. He moved almost effortlessly, but it seemed more real than anything he had ever experienced before. He paused, admiring the branches of a lush green almond tree that seemed oddly out of place.

The structures in the distance seemed like a wasteland of white stone. James couldn't discern much more than a multitude of blocks near the horizon of this vast desert. A bird flew overhead. A raven, perhaps? An eagle?

"Whoooooooo" The sound came from nowhere. *It couldn't have been the bird, could it?*

"WHOoooooooo" *maybe an owl?*

"WHOOOOOOOooooo" The sound came from all around James, making him jump.

"WHOOOOOOO ARE YOU?"

James woke up to Jess bouncing on his bed.

"Are you awake yet?" She smiled.

"Ugh, I am now. What's up, Jess?"

"I wanted to talk to you about the fight you had with those men. You saved us! How did you do that?"

"I don't know, the skill was just there, I guess."

"But how can that be? That's not normal. I mean, come on. How do you just know how to take on twenty guys without any problems?"

"Well I don't know, Jess. Maybe in my past I had some training or something, I'm not sure."

"Trained to do what? Kill people?"

"Maybe to defend people."

"Well, you certainly did that! But do you think you used to be a spy or something, like James Bond?"

"Who's James Bond?"

"You don't know who James Bon–" George walked in, cutting off Jess mid-sentence.

"Breakfast is ready."

"Let's go, Jess." James joined them in the kitchen.

"Good work last night," George said. "We reinforced the stilts quite well. They should hold for a good while,

"We all have families, James; they are all around us. We just have to see them."

"I don't understand."

"Because we are all a part of the same soul," Jess piped up.

"The same soul? How are we all a part of the same soul? Aren't we different?"

"Exactly. It is because we are all different that we are all the same." George said.

"The Great Soul is a creator with supreme awareness, but needs us to experience its' creations. It recreates itself and multiplies itself into everything you see before you. Nature, the universe, animals, and people. It is us, and we are it." Jessica spoke as though she had heard and repeated the story many times.

"So it creates itself continually? It always expands? Why?" He felt both confused and intrigued.

"Life will always go on; it is eternal, meaning there is no end or beginning. It just keeps repeating itself. Expanding, growing, changing."

"I see, but I'm not sure I completely understand."

"You will, James. We all will." George said.

"It's kids' stuff! We learn this when we're five years old." Jessica's dark brown eyes twinkled as she chuckled.

"George, you've been very kind to me, and I appreciate your beliefs and your culture but I think I have to find my own way. There's a lot I don't understand about who I am. How did I get here? Why can't I remember what happened for the first 30 years of my life? How come I have all these skills?" James said as they continued to eat their breakfasts.

"Indeed, you have many abilities. I don't quite understand them myself, and perhaps there are more you have yet to uncover but there must be a reason for it." George stopped eating and looked over at him.

"I'm sure there is. I'm sure there's a reason why all this is happening to me. Why do you keep telling me to forget about the South? What happened down there? What's going on in the world?" His breakfast was all but forgotten now.

"I prefer not to discuss such things in front of Jess. She's too young." George glanced sideways at Jessica who was rolling her eyes at his remark.

"Dad, I already know, it's okay. Kids talk too." He looked at her for a moment and his resolve fell as if he realized he couldn't protect her forever.

"Alright then, I will tell you what I know of what happened." George hung his head, took a deep breath, closed his eyes for a moment, and looked at James.

"What I will tell you is what I have heard, felt, and dreamed. I have not experienced this directly, none of us have. None of those who have left this place have ever returned." He paused, took another deep breath and continued. He told them that the last seven years had resulted in a total upheaval of society, and those in the southlands were under the control of a demon that had no remorse, a demon that destroyed indiscriminately. "He sees within you all that is dark and draws it out, breaks you down and becomes a part of you," George said. "Whatever this thing is, it isn't human, and we don't really know where it came from."

"You can't be serious, a demon?" James sat back in his chair, an eyebrow raised skeptically.

"Dad…?" Jessica stared at George, disbelief evident in her eyes.

"The world was a different place seven years ago, before the last great destruction. It was a symbol; he arrived here and had brought with him pure chaos. What followed was a monstrosity." George refused to meet James's eyes, or Jessica's.

"What the hell are you saying? That the world is run by some creature? I don't believe it!" James slammed his palm down on the table, making George and Jessica jump in alarm.

"Believe it, James. We live here in the North, deep within the snow because his mongrels freeze to death up here and can't reach us. We're safe, for the most part."

"What happened to the world?" James asked, crossing his arms.

George continued to explain that all the capital cities around the globe had been destroyed. Most governments had been caught completely off guard and almost all political officials were killed. Whole cities looked like they had been swallowed up by the earth. No one in the capitals had survived and at first people thought it was a terrorist action. "But it was nothing compared to what happened next."

"What happened?" James didn't want to know, but he knew he had to.

"People rose from the dead," George said. "They crawled and walked, mutating into something different altogether, something more fleshy and distorted. Some had no legs, like lumps of bone, muscle, and skin that moved with lightning speed."

George's haunted eyes stared at the table as he described the mutants. They ate people and they ate through cars. Some were still humanoid and banded together into twisted gangs hell-bent on torturing anyone they could find. They would lurk in the shadows and prey on the weak as they passed by, searching for victims. It seemed that hell had literally opened up and spewed madness into the streets.

"What was behind this? Is there any government left? Who runs the world? Tell me! Who runs the world?" James started to panic. Jessica put her hand on his arm in an effort to calm him down.

"We don't know where he comes from, or why he's here. We do what we can to survive in the world that remains but I cannot tell you who he is. We are told to never say his name."

"Who is it? You have to tell me."

"I can't say, James. The very mention of…" He looked down at his hands.

"You must tell me. Who has done this to us?" James pressed on.

"They call him Luzige." The room started spinning, James looked at George and everything began swirling. He couldn't see straight, his head was hurting. Then everything went black.

"Tamara! NOOOOOOO!"

"Ugh! What's going on?"

"What have you done to her? Where is she, damn you?"

"You will not find her. She is mine now!"

James' heart hurt. He tried to stand but the pain was so great that he stumbled and spun around, hitting his head on the table. He fell to the ground as if in slow motion. He saw them running towards him, Paul and Tamara. No, George and Jess. The darkness surrounded him until everything was black.

James was pulled into what felt like an embrace. He was sucked through a wind tunnel and then spat out on the other side. Before him sat a giant, at least one hundred feet tall, sitting in an ivory chair which took the form of tree trunks embedded into the earth. His limbs were many times the size of James's entire body. He sat by the entrance, looking like he was guarding it.

The portal behind him had been pitch black, but the room itself was completely white. The ceilings were a thousand feet tall, and James felt small in his six-foot-tall body beneath this red bearded giant.

"They are waiting for you, Lukman."

"What did you call me?"

"They are waiting for you in the cathedral. You must go now."

Instinctively James ran towards an adjacent room connected by a large ivory tree trunk. The tree trunk extended into several trees which were integrated into the architecture. Although he didn't know where he was, he was sure he was in the presence of a friend.

He felt warmth, acceptance, honour, and strength. *I am home.* Yet there was a sense of urgency in James' stride as he moved towards a room full of people he did not know.

The world around him was brilliantly lit by some unknown silvery light, which shimmered near the ceiling and rooftops. The light sparkled and danced around the windows more than anywhere else in the room. There was a sweet smell of flowers and the hushed sound of bells floating through the air.

There were twelve beings almost sixteen feet tall; they were surrounded by a bluish hue of energy and they wore robes of draconian origins with strange writing on their belts and collars. Their faces were barely visible and strangely dark when looked at from an angle, yet took on a mystical brilliance, a silver sparkling aura, when looked at straight-on.

James knew these beings somehow; they were important to him. They turned to him in unison and a flash overwhelmed him. He was reminded of training, of times in another world with friends and a woman, a beautiful woman who loved him. She stared at him from a distance before falling into a black abyss. He loved her. Her name was Tamara. James remembered darkness, then something took over. He felt cold and helpless, full of fear, doubt, and loneliness. *He's taken her.* James was rushed back into his body.

# THREE

## ORION

"JAMES... JAMES... WAKE up." His head hurt.

"Jess, what happened?" James attempted to get up. He was lying in bed, feeling very dazed.

"We talked in the kitchen, of the southlands, and then you fainted."

"Yes. I remember now. Something must have triggered my memories because some of them came back to me."

"Really? Like what?" Jess sat on the edge of the bed.

"I remember... I remember a woman named Tamara, and I remember a man named Paul, or Boulos. I remember... losing her." James stared at the ceiling as he spoke, processing the memories.

"Oh... I'm sorry." Jess squeezed his arm.

"It's not your fault. I don't even know what happened, Jess."

"Well, she must have been really important to you if you remembered her." Jess gave him a faint smile, which he returned.

"Yes, I suppose so."

"You've been asleep for a few hours already. I wanted to wake you to make sure you're okay; I was worried."

"Thank you, but I'm still feeling really exhausted. I think I'm going to rest more."

"Okay. I hope you feel better soon." She got up and gently closed the door behind her.

*Poor girl.* He knew she meant well, but he wasn't sure if he could be the friend she needed him to be. He couldn't stay. There was something inside of him, a burning desire for answers, and he couldn't turn his back on that. Within him there was a constant knowing that there was more, that this experience was just temporary. He couldn't understand why, but it must have had everything to do with his past, and without answers, the fire inside would consume him.

He lay there for a few more moments until he heard the door open again. It was George. He came in and motioned with his head if it was okay to enter.

"Come on in," James said as George sat on the foot of the bed.

"I've been dreaming of a woman. I see her repeatedly, I think she needs my help. She wore a shimmering dress of silver which glistened with different colours as she walked. She looked at me." James closed his eyes, trying to remember more.

"Do you know her name?"

"I think her name is Tamara, but I'm not sure. It's the same woman I've seen in previous dreams. There were others there, but I don't know their names. Except someone named Paul." James shrugged and looked down at the bedspread.

"Perhaps you should ask them. Maybe they'll respond."

"I don't know. It's possible. She looked almost lost this time. She just appears and vanishes, but it's always her, always the same woman."

"That means something, James." George patted his arm in support.

"What could it mean?" James looked at him, his brow furrowed in confusion.

"Only you can say: it's your dream. Perhaps she's someone from your past, or perhaps a guide."

"What kind of guide? What do you mean?"

"We all have spirit guides. They are friends that watch over us from the other side, the place we go to when we leave this world. They remind you of your path and assist you when needed."

"These guides, do they have access to all knowledge? Can they help restore my memories?"

"It's possible. Sit and think on this: you will find your helpers, and they will guide you to where you need to be."

"Thank you, George."

George smiled sadly. "Soon you will have to leave us. I have seen it. You will have to walk over the nine hills, and travel through the snake pit. You will have to leave everything behind, James. Sometimes you must be willing to lose it all, to get it all back. In the end, you will get everything back. I'm sure of it."

"What are you talking about?"

"You have been a good friend to me, and have helped my family. I thank you for that, but I know you must go." George squeezed his arm, much like Jessica had done earlier.

"Are you saying I have to leave? Why?"

"I am saying that others will need your help, and you must help them. I cannot keep you from this."

"I understand, but I don't want to leave. This is my home now."

"Your path will reveal itself in time, I'm sure. Just think about it, and rest for a while. There's no need for you to go anywhere tonight. I need to fix the car if you're going to go anywhere at all."

"Thanks, George, I appreciate it." George smiled at his friend, got up, and left the room.

James lay back down, and as his head hit the pillow, he had a sinking feeling, as if he was drowning. The room became dark. His body began to vibrate, and his heart beat faster. Everything was happening so fast, and he couldn't stop it. He was drifting away.

James was pulled through a vortex of light and sound. An inner voice spoke to him.

*You will soon understand.*

James arrived in a grassy knoll of beautiful green. He had not seen green grass before. All he could recall were the snowy hills around George and Jess's village. This place seemed foreign but at the same time like home. It was more real than real life. His senses were alive; he felt each blade of grass. He saw trees of green with rose blossoms and a lake in the distance which shimmered with all the colours of the rainbow.

The beauty around him was astonishing; the people around him were glowing with energy. Their faces were bright with smiles and love as they somehow imprinted him with thoughts of greetings. They moved fast, walking by without stopping. James walked forward, thinking this must be some kind of dream, so why not play along? Yet this dream seemed like another world.

A man approached from the distance, wearing a white shirt, brown pants and shoes. Respectable looking clothes, but he seemed relaxed instead of business-like. Although he was still at a distance, James could gaze directly into his eyes as if he were right in front of him. They were sharp, with streaks of brown and green; wise, loving eyes that were somehow familiar. He had a white beard that matched his neatly parted hair. He continued to walk toward James, who was imprinted with the word *Orion*. The man's name was Orion.

"Do not be afraid," Orion said. "Welcome, James. We call this place The Summerlands. I am Orion. You do not remember me, but I am an old friend." He was roughly James's height, with a rounded jaw. Solidly built, but still friendly.

"Why am I here? What's this all about?"

"To put it into terms you'd understand: you've travelled to a different universe. Our universe is less dense than yours; we are more energy than matter here. But more importantly, I've been waiting for you. We all have."

"What do you mean?"

"We have been awaiting your return to our realm. We were not sure if you'd be able to return to our world after you donned a new physical form. We worked diligently to construct it for you—your body, that is.

This is rarely done, you see, in multi-verse travel. We were not even sure if you'd come back to us."

"Multi-verse? New form?" James looked at him, his confusion evident.

Orion told him he was under the veil of third dimensional amnesia. He said James' energy matrix took on a new physical form in the third dimension when he started over with a new life, like everyone's energy matrix did. It meant James forgot everything that happened in his previous life. "But," Orion said, "You can overcome it and recall who you were. This is the second and most recent form you've taken in order to stop the invasion. Your first experience was as Jacob Cross, a brilliantly ambitious scientist. You were born, raised, and educated. You had a girlfriend and a fantastic career. Unfortunately, that career lead to the height of the world's turmoil, and you died. Since then, seven years have passed.

"Jacob had helped to create something in that life, something that hadn't existed in his realm since long before your recorded history, when civilization was at its truest peak. It was a headset that worked with certain tone and sound frequencies, reminiscent of Atlantean power. Using it caused a link within you.

"Orion, none of what you are saying makes sense. Just answer me this simple question: Who am I now? What's this all about?"

"That is a grand question indeed, and a question only you can answer. What I'll tell you is that you're an entity, like me. An energy matrix combined with a belief construct or perspective that results in your personality. You are a multi-dimensional consciousness with the power to change and manifest forms, traverse realms, shape-shift, and even recreate yourself using any host body you need in any particular dimension."

"What the hell are you talking about?" James yelled. He was tired of being confused and feeling as if he was being kept in the dark.

"Listen!" Orion shouted. "For now, you are James. You were not born into the physical world as you understand it. An energy vortex was created, and your physical body was willed into being, allowing your consciousness to bond with it. This was the only way you could get back to the earth realm so quickly after you were murdered. Even though we started work immediately on your new body, it took years to complete the process. Nearly seven years have passed since you died as Jacob." He spoke calmly and patiently.

"So I've been dead for seven years." James closed his eyes, trying to let that information sink in.

"You, as a being, can never die. You only change forms. A more accurate statement is that you were absent from the physical realm for seven years, but you've returned, donning a new body after your first one was destroyed." Orion began walking towards a nearby fountain and motioned for James to follow.

"Wait a minute. There's something you're not telling me."

Orion looked at him sternly. "What are you talking about?"

"I'm talking about you and all of this. There's more to it, isn't there? Something you don't want me to know. I can sense it."

"Don't be ridiculous. I'm telling you all that I know." Orion removed his white vest. James tried to make out the gold lettering embossed on the back but he wasn't quite able to.

"I died as Jacob, correct?"

"Yes." He cupped the water from the fountain and washed his well-muscled arms before motioning James forward.

"What are you doing?"

"Receive a blessing; this fountain is pure source energy." As the water spread over his arms, it was somehow absorbed into his skin.

"There is something else. How many times have I done this? How many times have I tried to stop him?"

He looked at James and gave a slight smile.

"This is the seventh time I've tried to stop him, isn't it?"

"Remarkable."

"What?"

"You weren't nearly as perceptive in your previous lives."

"Why aren't you telling me the truth?"

"Because it doesn't benefit you to know right now. We shouldn't speak of it."

"It does benefit me. I need to know what went wrong."

"Maybe you should know. This is your seventh time doing this, and if we don't succeed this time, existence as we know it will end."

"As in, life on Earth?"

"No. *All* of life. In all dimensions, across all universes, and through all of time. Gone."

"How can this be?"

"While you were away, an evil demon was able to enter the earth realm, bond with a body, and eventually began to take over. Most nations have already fallen to his will. But he's not just evil; he's the antithesis to creation itself, the Omega. If this being is allowed to destroy this earth dimension—your world—then it will ignite a chain reaction that will spread like a virus, undoing all creation."

"You're speaking of Luzige, right? If he is allowed to conquer earth, he will destroy all that is?"

"All relative universes in creation will be destroyed. What is called God will still exist, but only in the realm of the absolute. But our relative experience…our individualized experiences will cease to be."

"Who did he bond with?" James asked.

"He bonded with Edward Aidan, the CEO of Netex, and the corporation that sponsored the development of the Auditum Technology—your creation. He was manipulated from a young age by these evil forces, and was slowly twisted into a perfect mold for Luzige's possession."

"Why him? Why not someone else?"

"Like you, he was extremely receptive to psychic phenomenon. Unfortunately, a series of horrific events turned him against the world, and he willingly gave permission to Luzige to take over his body in hopes of gaining further power."

"How can I stop him? He killed me once, and now…now I don't remember anything."

"This time is different. You are different. The link you have allows you to tap in to the source." Orion gave a hint of a smile.

"The source?" James asked.

"The source is the databanks, or libraries, of all knowledge and power. This fountain here is pure source. Drink it, wash it over yourself; it's pure creative energy. Where Luzige must survive on the fear generated by others, you have access to infinite power. Even though the power of fear can be very strong, especially with so many giving their power away, it pales in comparison to what you will be able to do." He said that the relative dimensions relied on a balance of love and individualization, but if Luzige started tipping the scales by making humans produce more fear than love, creation would cease to be. "The dream would be over."

"What do you mean?"

"Just understand this: there are an infinite number of possible experiences to be had within creation. They are endless. And when you tap in, you understand the experiences of others completely. This allows you to access abilities and skills from countless different dimensions and lifetimes. Surely you've already noticed your uncanny abilities that just happen in times of duress?"

"Yes, I've noticed. It was as if I had immediate access to the information I needed. Sometimes the information stayed with me and sometimes it didn't. It was only there when I needed it."

"Precisely. We've never established such a connection before in the earth realms. You will be well equipped for what's to come, I assure you."

"Why do I have all these abilities?"

"There is something unique in you, a vortex of energy within your core. This unique vortex allows access to other dimensions of thought, experience, and pure knowing. It is in your moments of need that you access this vortex."

"Why do I have this vortex? Where did it come from?"

"It came from using Auditum— the headset you created. This caused a vibrational shift within you, raising your consciousness and resulting in many changes within you, the least of which is the ability to travel here. And once your consciousness expands, it is very hard to change it back to what it was before."

"So where am I, really? You call this place the Summerlands, but is this a different planet? Are we on an alternate earth?" The place, after all, was so much more vivid than anything James had ever experienced.

"The answer to all of that is yes. Yes this is a different planet, something similar to earth. The question is what vibration? We are in a very high dimensional plane, something like the seventh dimension of existence, if you will. This is where your consciousness primarily resides when not with a body. This is because you are at a particularly high level of consciousness."

Orion said that the vortex was how they were able to communicate so freely with James. It was a channel they used to enter into his consciousness, which was also where his abilities mainly came from. The skills and information were all accumulated with his past lives. "At times you may access this information easily, and other times you do not. Do you understand this?" Orion paused.

James nodded. "Go on."

"For the purposes of this explanation, you're in a state of amnesia in your physical body. This is a state imposed by the reality matrix you have entered called the third dimension, as I've said. Upon entering this dimension, you forget all aspects of who you are. You do this in order to wipe the slate clean, to start over and create yourself anew. This is the purpose of the third dimension. This is always done for the purpose of evolution. When you are finished with your creation and your new personality, you will then be able to access your previous experiences to get a better grasp of who you are. It will then benefit you to have this information as you plan your next cycle of experience."

"You've lost me," James said.

"I understand that this will be hard to grasp, but for now try to understand that you are much bigger than your body, even much bigger than the confines of your own mind."

"Okay, so I'm in a state of amnesia which is why I can't remember the first 30 years of my life?"

"No, not exactly."

"Well, what does it mean then?" James snapped.

"What I'm about to tell you may seem hard to believe, but try to understand that all things are possible through awareness. If you understand the simple mechanics behind the magic show, the trick is no longer a trick. You simply need to understand that all things are possible, all things are attainable, and you just need the light to show you the way."

"I'm tired of you dancing around my questions. Why can't I remember the first 30 years of my life?"

"Because they never existed."

"What?"

"On Earth, you were once known as a different person. In that life, you were betrayed and killed. We knew that may be a possible outcome for you. We couldn't have known what would follow for the earth realm or that so many would suffer." Orion lowered his head, sorrow flickering over his face, as if he was thinking about some atrocity but holding back the details.

"What outcome?" James asked.

"Once we became aware of your murder on earth, we immediately prepared your new vessel for your re-entry into the third dimension. This was all part of your 'Time of Choosing,' all part of the plan. You knew that you may not survive and the probability of your death was very high for that life path but you also knew that you needed to return to finish what you had set out to do. This is rarely done, re-entry of this nature, but sometimes we have to adapt. We weren't sure if we could pull it off honestly, and we needed support from The Enclave to accomplish it." James stared at Orion in complete amazement. *Maybe I didn't have a past as James, maybe I was first Jacob, and now in a new incarnation.* He began to lose his sense of self and grew agitated.

"We could only manifest the body in the far north, far away from Luzige and his spies. It was our best shot at getting you back to earth without detection." Orion continued on, keeping his voice calm. He knew James was beginning to lose control.

"Why can't he detect me?" James said, his voice shaking.

"He can't recognize your energy or your appearance. He is convinced that he has destroyed you, so for now we have the element of surprise. It's your best means of protection."

"Then why not allow me to remember everything, all at once, right now?" James clenched his fists and tried to control his frustration and panic.

"There will be a time where not having your past will serve you. You may not understand now but that's okay. This amnesia can be useful. You see, the more you remember, the more he will sense your presence in his dimension. This cannot be avoided, but if you can accomplish what is needed without drawing attention to yourself, then we may have an advantage. We also need to pace ourselves. If he detects your presence yet you are not prepared, then he will destroy you."

"Is this why I don't remember anything about being Jacob? My slate has been wiped clean?"

"Yes. It's really only through this amnesia that we are able to hide you from him for so long. Too much awareness of Luzige will bring him forth, too much remembrance of Jacob will attract his attention, and you are *not* ready for that yet."

James nodded, finally understanding a little. "How does the amnesia affect my energy?"

"By entering with a body, you are forced to experience this amnesia. Your beliefs create your perspective; your perspective creates your next thought which shapes your actions and experience. These beliefs, thoughts, and actions resonate uniquely, and are the core of your individuality. When your beliefs match those of Jacob, the energy signature and frequency will be unmistakable to him."

"So is Jacob who I truly am?"

"Jacob's consciousness was only a small aspect of who you are. You are much greater than that. But I know what you're asking. The manifestation of Jacob was a very high vibration indeed, and now you are most likely vibrating at a lower rate, thus avoiding detection. Your memories will be fragmented, but that's okay because we are here to help when the time comes, hopefully in the near future. Your dreams will be filled with as much information as we can provide without drawing too much attention."

"Are these dreams real?"

"You've been a warrior for many lifetimes, and that is truly your nature," Orion said. "You are also a great teacher but that truth is yours to discover, and I've already said too much. If we are to have any chance of stopping him, you'll need to unlock your power through use of the Auditum headset."

"How can Auditum help me?"

"You will need this technology to fine tune your vibration. You don't understand how to access your power consciously yet, and this technology can tune you into higher frequencies than you can hope to achieve with your physical body alone. With the right guidance, you could move mountains with it. And, as your world has discovered, it could destroy them as well. As Jacob, you barely scratched the surface of Auditum's power, but you now have the opportunity to unlock its unlimited potential."

"Tell me more about this technology," James said, fascinated.

"As Jacob, you were born with this science in you because you had spent previous lives in Atlantis. You remembered these concepts and technologies, bringing them to life in your work at Netex Corporation. At certain frequencies, the headset technology unlocked advanced abilities of the brain, essentially lifting the veil between realities. At times, it even caused objects to appear out of thin air. In other instances, it was used as a highly hypnotic mind control device. Not long after your defeat, Auditum hit the streets and nearly destroyed society overnight."

"What happened?"

"Horrific creatures walked across nearly every metropolis. The earth was overrun by them as they pillaged cities. We believe that Luzige used Auditum to open portals, allowing these creatures through. Or possibly they were mutations caused by the Netex Catalyst drug, a mutagenic agent that affects the pineal and pituitary glands. That's what caused the mutations." Orion looked fierce.

"We placed you far away from civilization, by a nice family we knew would help you, and whom you would help in return. Pay attention to your dreams from now on. They will guide you to other friends who will help you remember."

"I'll do my best then."

"We do not have the luxury of time, James; we need you to complete your journey in order for this realm to survive. *He* is moving fast, and this realm is but a step on his path to the complete destruction of creation."

James's eyes widened.

"Do not be afraid," Orion said. "We'll talk again soon. It's time to wake up, now."

# FOUR

## A Traveler

A GUST OF WIND blew through the window as James opened his eyes. The sun shone through, creating a beam of almost mystical light. A shiver went up his spine in sync with the wind, and a solemn feeling of foreboding overtook him.

James remembered Orion. Maybe he was right and James didn't actually have a past before meeting George and Jess. Maybe he did come out of nowhere. Knowing these things changed him. He cared for his new family, but he felt detached from them at the same time.

Fragments of his former life flashed through his mind, especially those with Tamara. He felt a connection to her. In many of his dreams she had long brown hair, a thin yet strong feminine shape, and bold mysterious brown eyes. She wore a sun dress and she pulled James in when she smiled, but that wasn't often. Most of his images of her show a saddened, lost girl, deeply hurt.

George knocked at the door. "James, are you awake?"

"Yes. Come in."

"I've been worried about you. You blacked out for nearly a day. You were rambling, or rather shouting. You mentioned some names before you collapsed. Sounded like Tamra, or Tamara… Tarif. Something like that. Do you remember?"

"I remember saying the names, I remember collapsing, and I remember having a very long and crazy dream."

"Oh? What kind of dream?"

"I was sucked through a tunnel and arrived in a beautiful grassy park with gardens. It was incredible, and felt so real. I talked to a man named Orion; he said he was an old friend. He told me a lot of things, and some of it matches what you said at the breakfast table."

"So you're a traveler too? What other talents do you have?"

"A traveler?"

"Yes, that's what my people call folk like us."

"Folk like us? People with crazy dreams?"

"Perhaps they aren't so crazy. Go on, tell me the rest."

"He told me that most major cities have been destroyed. Is that true?"

George said that was what he had heard. After the mutants started destroying everything and killing each other, people escaped the cities and grouped into smaller communities up north to stay alive. They lost communications a few years ago, but he doubted that any form of government that wasn't under Luzige's control had been re-established.

"So there's no government?" James said, surprised. Even though there hadn't been any mention of it before, he had always assumed there was one.

"People govern themselves mostly. There are good and bad people everywhere…some really bad. We just work in order to survive. People in general are about the same regardless of the conditions. There are good folk and bad folk. We try to steer clear of the bad folk."

"So the communications just got cut off?"

"Our yearly shipment of food was stopped and since then we've relied on hunting and fishing. Now we know next to nothing about what's happening down there."

"Why did people start mutating?"

"Catalyst," said George. "A chemical called Catalyst was released into the water, which started causing mutations. No one knows for sure why he poisoned the water, but people thought it was just to cause chaos and fear."

"There isn't much left of society now. Cities are very dangerous; no one gets in or out. Those things will feast on you out there."

James shook his head in disbelief. "Orion also told me I wasn't born here, that I wasn't born at all. He said I just appeared the day you found me."

"The day we found you was a strange day indeed. We thought you might have come from the sky, but who could survive a fall like that? Something is special about you, James, and I have no idea why you can do the things you can do. You know electronics and technology like you're an engineer, you can pick up information out of thin air, and you can fight like I've never seen before. And now you're a traveler."

"What does it mean to be a traveler?"

"My people have been known to travel out of the body. Many use this form of travel to shape change into different animals. Travelers often have experiences similar to yours where we talked to our old friends from the other worlds, and what you describe sounds like the same. It's rare that someone comes back with such clarity, as these dreams are fleeting." James could hear the sincerity in George's voice. "You should trust Orion," he said.

"Then I have to go south. You were right; I have something to do with all of this. I don't really know why, but somehow I'm connected to it. Maybe I can stop him."

"I don't think you understand what you're up against. Luzige rounded up thousands of people to personally torture, going through them one by one. The military and police either joined forces with him or disbanded. There are small rebel groups, but nothing has made a dent in his armies. He rules the world with an iron fist, and there is no going back."

"You're right, there is no going back. But that doesn't mean we can't stop all of this. Thank you for helping me."

George sighed. "You're welcome. I'll help you in any way I can." He put his arm on James's shoulder and smiled.

"Thank you again, George." He smiled at his friend and patted him on the shoulder.

"I think you should rest some more. You have a long journey ahead of you."

"I'll see you in the morning."

"Good night." George got up and closed the door behind him.

James sat on his bed for a moment, looking out at the sky and wondering what his journey had in store. He thought about how much more he now remembered, and how much more he knew. But without understanding who he was, how could he know how to put an end to all of this madness?

He lay back down, quieted his mind, and drifted off to sleep.

James found himself in an old library, one with many books on wall-to-wall shelves. There was a straw hat on a table in the middle of the room. Beside it was an old pair of glasses, round with wire frames. There was an open book as well, which he noticed as he moved closer to the table. The book was large with pictures and words in dark ink. Both pictures and words were swimming on the page, as if the book was alive. As he got closer to the book, it spoke, like many voices whispering.

*The words of his choosing are at hand. The actions will come and there will be none. The smoke will shadow the innocent, and the serpents will come, their fury unstoppable. Only the unified spirit can...* James got up and turned around to see a rather large monk standing behind him.

"Ah, you must be James. Do you remember me? No, of course you don't. You don't remember anyone, do you? That's rather convenient for everyone, I gather. I think you have found something interesting, no?" The monk snatched the book off the table.

"You mean the book?"

"Yes, of course."

"It spoke to me."

"The Orb tends to do that. How did you arrive here, James? This is my sanctuary." He said, walking away.

"I don't know, I fell asleep and ended up here." James figured it was just another one of his travelling dreams. He followed the monk as he scurried around the library.

"You expect me to believe you fell asleep and just ended up here? You must be mad. This is not a random coincidence. Perhaps you were sent here. In fact, there is no such thing as coincidence; all things have purpose. You must be here for a purpose, a reason, a mission, in fact. Yes, a mission. Do you know your mission?"

"I don't know of any mission. Like I said, I..."

He walked away from James again, ignoring him. He moved rather briskly with sharp movements, almost demonic in fact. He shuffled towards the book shelf, then another, then another. He was searching for something at an extremely fast pace, his thick, sack-like robe moving with a heavy weight. His eyes glowed as he searched the shelves. His hair and face made him look rather old, but he moved with lightning speed.

"Ahh, found it. Here it is: the book I've been looking for. Do you know what this is? No, of course you don't. What a pity it must be: no memory, no destiny, and no identity. How do you function when you don't even know who you are?"

"It seems like you know things about me, but I have no idea who you are."

"I am Lucious. I am a guide, sometimes a teacher, sometimes other things. You knew me once, long ago. This is my library, or my home, my reality. Whatever you want to call it. Yes, I know some things about you, as there seems to be some information floating about the realms. You are 'Galanic' it seems, much to everyone's surprise. You are a three part being, a very rare creature. I have heard you might be one of the three I seek. I was told there would be three; he said it would be so. That's why you've come. That's your purpose."

"He who? What the hell are you talking about?"

"Indeed. You are somebody that I used to know, and that is why you are here, isn't it? You have come for knowledge as you once had in the past. Let me look closer at you." He grabbed James's face, inspecting it like a master acquiring a prize horse. He leaned in and sniffed.

"Yes. I think it is you. Your eyes are different, though; they look fake. But then again, I'm very different as well. I never thought I'd see you again. Not after what happened to you and your friends. He was merciless." The monk grinned slightly.

"What happened to me, Lucious? I don't know where I am or what I'm supposed to be doing. You need to give me some answers. What's a Galanic?"

"You have three distinct aspects to your consciousness. Each has a role, a purpose as defined by your Over soul. It was only after your... unfortunate end that I came to understand the larger plan. You see, a Galanic is a certain type of being that cannot be trapped as easily as other souls."

"Who was I?"

"You were once known as Jacob. You were the rational one, the logical mind in that expression. The analytical personality of your three part being."

"The rational one? Then what am I now?"

"That remains to be seen, but from what I can tell this personality might be the warrior."

"The warrior?" It seemed about right with all the skills I unknowingly possessed.

He started leafing through the book he grabbed from the shelf. He motioned for his glasses and James grabbed them. "Ah here it is," he said, putting on the glasses. "The Galanic Psyche. As the manifestation of warrior power, you potentially have access to many great abilities and knowing. It says here that you may even bend energy and time to your will. Hmm, but this remains to be seen doesn't it?"

"What does?"

"Whether or not you are the warrior."

"If I'm not that then what else could I be? What's the third part of my consciousness?"

"It doesn't say." He closed the book abruptly and smiled.

"Tell me more about Jacob."

"As Jacob, you were brilliant; you invented a technology which bridged the gap between dimensions. You used this technology to tap in, and shift into different perspectives and dimensions of experience. A technology far beyond anything created on your planet for thousands of years."

"Only thousands of years?" James raised an eyebrow. "Does that mean that a civilization had this technology and then lost it?"

"Sound is a very powerful technology. All matter is just a vibration; all vibration is a form of sound. One of the most powerful in physical reality in fact, is the power of sound. Sound can greatly modify your consciousness, which itself is simply a vibration of energy. Yes, there were other ancient civilizations with technologies like this, who literally destroyed themselves. You might know of Atlantis and Lemuria."

"Yes."

"Since the loss of those civilizations, no one has tapped into those higher frequencies. Until Jacob Cross invented the Auditum headset."

"What happened to him after that?"

According to Lucious, Jacob had invented a portal for consciousness using the Auditum sound waves. This allowed Luzige to enter Earth. He manipulated Edward Aidan into letting him possess his body. Luzige was next to impossible to destroy after entering a body. Jacob came close to defeating him, but ended up getting destroyed in the process.

"How do you know all this?" James asked.

"I helped you once. I can help you again I think. I will help you find your friends; I know you are looking for them. Aren't you?"

"I'm looking for a woman named Tamara."

"Of course you are. She is in the Abyss. A realm where Luzige toys with souls, and feeds off their energy. Yes, I can help you find your friends. I will send you to them. I think you should go now. I'll guide you to them, I promise." His eyes began to glow a bright smoky blue, and he smiled a wide grin that set off red flags in James's head.

He felt a tugging, then an electrical charge followed by a shift, and he was immediately transported to another place. Somewhere large and infinitely vast. Marble structures were everywhere along with massive buildings, many times larger than the pyramids on earth. Beings of light flowed in the sky at great speeds and in all directions. James stood upon a massive staircase which led to the largest temple he had ever seen or could have ever imagined. It stood hundreds, perhaps thousands of feet tall, and its connected buildings were all he could see in either direction. He started walking up the steps, admiring the massive structures, the magnificent design which was reminiscent of Roman architecture.

In the distance stood a large fountain statue of a warrior holding a massive sword of shimmering light and steel in one hand. Sparkling water poured from the other hand into the river below.

James felt a familiar presence beside him. He turned and saw Orion, who smiled, glowing with an inviting light. "Welcome back," Orion said.

"Thank you. I'm not sure how I got here, but based on our last discussion I guess I should have expected it. I met someone named Lucious."

"Ah, yes, Lucious. He certainly has turned a little eccentric since your return. But it is his process, and we give him his space."

"He told me what happened to me and how I was killed. He also told me about Luzige, like you did, and he came to be. Why is this so? Why do we do the things that we do? How was he created?"

"Why don't we go to the hall of records and see if we can find the answers to your questions? We might gain the proper perspective on what we've accomplished thus far and what we are trying to achieve. This might help your remembering…"

"Why do they call me Lukman here?" There were so many names he didn't understand.

"Have you forgotten the name given to you by creation itself? On earth, I was Jacob's father, Alan. In this place I use my true name Orion. Most will call you by your true name, Lukman."

"You were my father?" A flood of memories came to light. Memories of him playing games with his father and times growing up. "Dad?"

"Yes. It's me, Jake."

"Thank you for being here with me."

"That's what we do, Jake, we help each other, lifetime after lifetime."

"There's something you need to know if you're going to stop him. We created Luzige. We feed fear into our societies, and that fear has created him. The pain that we inflict upon each other only serves his purpose more fully. He is also the cause for much destruction during our time on earth. He was the whisper in the ear of many murders and rapists, the devil on the shoulder of the simple- and weak-minded. He has created much destruction through us, and we are to blame for this." Orion paused so James could process the information.

"So we have failed to learn the most important lesson of all, then: to live in harmony, and reject fear, and all emotions that stem from it."

"That is correct, but the pressing matter of our time is at hand. You, Lukman, have taken on the responsibility to confront Luzige with the help from those left with enough awareness and strength to stop him. Luzige will use up and destroy the earth, then proceed to the next planet in our solar system with life on it and devour all of life in that dimension. Then he'll move onto the next, but with nothing to stop him. Our last stand is here. Now. The time for your reckoning is at hand, and we need you to stop him before it's too late."

"And if I fail?"

"Then all is lost. But we will have our memory of the beauty we had created, of the love we shared, of the times we spent together. Do you remember when we used to play together when you were a boy?"

"Yes, I do."

"Those memories will not leave us. Even when we merge back into the oneness, we will always remember each other and the love we shared together."

"Then all is not lost."

"No."

"Then I'll go back and finish what I started," James said. "How do we begin?"

"There are some souls who want to meet you before you go." Orion spoke as they walked along a small path.

"You were once a little boy, but you are no longer that anymore. That doesn't mean you were never a boy. It is simply an aspect of your being. Whether or not you choose to identify with it is entirely up to you."

They walked for a while, over hills of lustrous green grass and radiant trees that smelled of sweet dew. Each held a slight glow about them, like the subtle heat rising from a stone yet shimmering with different colours. James noticed what looked like a mighty oak tree and walked towards it. His fingers tingled when he touched the rough bark. A feeling shot through his heart, then flooded the rest of his being with perfect light and electrical impulses. He was one with this wise giver of life. He could feel its unbending faith and the security in its roots, in a deep knowing of what it was, a confidence firmly planted in the fact that it is a part of all that is. If only James was so firmly rooted. He looked back at Orion with a warm sentiment and knew that there was the possibility they may never meet again.

"I will leave you here. I will be back for you when you've seen what you needed to see. She will be waiting for you," Orion said.

"How will I know what I must do?" James asked.

"Just search for your next move and you will be guided. When you return to Earth, you'll learn more about your past self as Jacob. This will come in time, I assure you." Orion spoke, squeezing James's shoulder to show he believed in him.

"Why are my memories clouded?"

"You're still dazed by this experience, but if we didn't take this route, you would have to be reborn to a woman, and we would have to wait for you to mature. We just didn't have the time for that, so we improvised. It is rarely done this way, but we managed."

"What could have happened?"

"The body would have arrived on earth without you at the helm."

"But I'm saving time this way?"

"Yes. Right now, in this state you are slightly out of phase, so to speak. You are neither in our dimension, nor in theirs. You are able to travel between both, materializing in either realm as you choose."

James's brow furrowed. "I don't understand."

"Your memories are clouded, as you have not gone through the proper healing and therapy that is normally performed when an individual dies. If you had, you would recall not only who you truly are but also all of your previous lifetimes. Yet, you would lose your connection to the body entirely. But in this life, you have chosen this way in order to live a full life in two bodies: Jacob and now James. It is through this separation and union that you will free earth and stop Luzige."

"What is Luzige, exactly?"

"We don't know. We only know that he's ancient, one of the original creations from long ago. It is possible he was created to devour realms. Others think he is simply an entity created by humanity with every act of indignity that they allow. He is the dark side of their consciousness, the side that they refuse to acknowledge. Perhaps these acts of pure negativity amassed enough energy to become consciously aware, creating Luzige himself."

"How did this energy become aware?"

"With enough concentration, energy will explode with consciousness. The human race allowed so many acts of violence and negativity to occur that the energy they had collected became more aware and grows stronger. This entity, Luzige, feeds on fears and negativity, which is now in an almost inexhaustible supply on Earth."

"Why was this allowed in creation? Has God created this?" Orion remained silent, looking across the still waters nearby. "Did God create Luzige?" James asked.

"It's possible. It's also very plausible that creation gave humanity the power to create as well as to destroy. If God allows you the intelligence to create a bomb, do you blame him when it explodes and you perish? They have been given the power to create anything they can imagine and thus they are the creators of either their bliss or their destruction. And in order to preserve our creations which hold value, we must stop Luzige or the physical dimensions will perish."

James nodded. "What's my next step?"

"Come, I have something to show you."

# FIVE

## THE GREAT WATER

ORION TOOK JAMES into a towering castle of grey and white stone, which resembled an early mosque or temple. The outer cloister was decorated with a statue of a strong warrior woman holding a golden sword. The name Anza came to James, along with a sensation of peace when he looked at her. James followed Orion to the large wooden doors which towered over twenty feet tall. Carved upon it were angels engaged in a dance. They appeared to slowly twirl within the door itself.

The doors opened, revealing a room perhaps one hundred times the size of the outer appearance of the temple. They walked towards the centre of the room where several people were occupied with something that looked like a large globe perhaps five feet across and encased in a cylinder which supported it. The orbs appeared to be glowing, shimmering with a light blue hue, and the people were interacting with the technology. James and Orion approached a vacant orb.

"Welcome to the City of Pandium. The temple name refers to an ancient word meaning all experience. Here you can view and experience your previous incarnations, and here you'll understand the importance of stopping Luzige by witnessing what he's done. Hopefully, you'll learn how to stop him in the process."

"Can I view the experience of Jacob here as well? Or my current experience?"

"No, you cannot, not here. We will deal with that later. Place your hands on the orb."

"Where will you be?"

"I'll wait here, but what happens next is up to you."

James took a deep breath. "Here goes nothing," he muttered, and he was transported to another place and time.

James walked into what looked like a pyramid made of white tapestry and engraved with ancient carvings of a language similar to Aramaic, which he could somehow read. *GO HE WHO ENTERS WITHIN WITH PEACE AND FORGIVENESS.*

*Perhaps a message to those who may not like what they see. Perhaps, something more,* James thought.

The tall, deep brown doors swung open to greet him. There were rows and rows of shelves containing scrolls and old books. Souls floated high above, perhaps hundreds of feet in the air. They were reading books and wearing loose fitting clothing similar to togas or robes. There were hundreds of souls amidst hundreds of thousands of shelves. Some flew from shelf to shelf, but most were motionless, absorbed in whatever book they were reading. At the very top of the structure was a glass domed roof, supported by a brass framing that was similar to a wheel spoke.

By instinct, James willed himself into the air, letting something pull him upwards towards a bookshelf suspended in mid-air in the centre of the room. He slowed and looked into one of the aisles, seeing only books and light on the other side. He floated through the aisle, moving slowly and examining the endless books around him, until he saw her, her entire body radiating in white and gold light. She was thumbing through a book, her loose flowing dress and veil fluttering in some slight breeze. She looked at him and gave him a welcoming smile, the aura of love around her pulling James in. He moved closer, unable to help himself.

"You look lost. Have you come here looking for something?" She spoke in a soft, musical voice.

"I don't know."

"The best time to find things is when you don't know them. But you look like you've come here with a purpose. Is there a particular life book you're looking for? Perhaps one of the book of realms?"

"I don't know what those are."

"A book of realms is a biopic of the entire history of a reality frequency: all that is, was, or shall be. A life book is the story of one's life, from birth to death, every thought that crossed your mind, every emotion, or context for your decisions. Every experience of yours that has ever occurred."

"Are there no private moments?"

"No."

"Why?"

"Do you keep things from yourself?"

"I don't know."

"Well perhaps you're here to find out."

"Who are you?"

"My name is Vivian. I come here from time to time. I enjoy reading; it helps me stay grounded."

"I don't quite understand what all of this is."

"You are new here; you've just come from the body and you haven't received your reunification. No wonder you're so tired and confused. Do you remember your family in the body?"

"I remember my father. My mother left us when I was very young and I don't recall much of her," James said. "My father was with a woman named Kate for many years. She was like a mother to me."

Did your father ever speak to you of your real mother?"

"Only bits and pieces. He had an old picture of her in her wedding dress, looking out the window. That's the only memory I have of what she looked like. My father said she left us, and I never asked why."

Vivian smiled sadly. "She was very sick when you were a baby, and she died of leukaemia not long after your first birthday. She loved you very much, and she still does."

James looked away. "Why are you telling me this? How do you know?"

"Because I *was* your birth mother. My name was Gloria."

"You were my birth mother?"

"Yes. You had a brother as well, who's still alive. His name is Joshua."

"A brother? Why didn't I know about this?"

"Because your father couldn't raise two children at once and put one up for adoption. It was a difficult decision, but it was to give both of you your best chances."

"Where is he now?"

"The province took over custody after he was put up for adoption. He stayed in the foster system until he was eighteen, and then joined the army. He is very much like you, but he needs your help. He will not know you as his brother, especially when you return. You will be different; your face will be similar but not the same, and your eyes will have changed, an effect of not being born by a woman."

"So you're telling me the same thing. I just appeared out of nothingness."

"Is that so hard to believe? This is the place where all things come: the nothingness first, then thought and then creation."

"I don't understand what I must do next."

"Yours is only the decision to act, if you think the world is worth saving. If you think what you have in your present reality is worth saving at all, then you will do what you must. But creation does not require anything of its creations."

"But what about Luzige? Won't he destroy everything?"

"No. He too will be absorbed back into the oneness from whence he came because he too is an aspect of creation. Once physical creation has ended, he too will be absorbed back into the totality of the universe."

"Then why do we fight? What is the purpose in recreating myself in order to confront this demon? I don't understand any of this."

Vivian explained that creation, or life, was divided up into segments. Each segment of reality was divided by frequency, going from the physical world to the astral world, to the Etheric world, and so on. Each universe was divided by frequency. All of it was an aspect of duality. In the realms of duality, everyone could have individual lives even though they all belonged to the same consciousness. The Auditum technology was what Jacob used to travel to different realms.

"Auditum was able to move me between realities? To here?"

"Yes, you were able to move here with Auditum, to the Astral Realms. This place is why the technology was so sought after. Imagine the knowledge that can be accessed using Auditum. Unlimited knowledge can be used for good, but it can also be used for selfish gain."

She told him that there were realms where all life was one, but there were also realms that had the illusion of separation, like in the Astral Realms. It was the realms of separation that were in danger. "Ultimate reality is never in danger, and in essence, neither are you," she said.

"What do you mean I'm never in danger? I just died."

"You still exist, don't you? You changed forms. Your body as Jacob died but you still exist. It still feels as real as it did on Earth, does it not?" Vivian moved slowly to another book, taking it gently from the library shelf.

"Yes, maybe more so. My senses seem much sharper here than they did on Earth. It is so much more unlimited here."

"Earth is the dream and reality is here, with your spiritual families. Let me ask you something: do you feel any guilt associated to your life as Jacob? Any remorse?"

"No, not really. Although I'm sure that my answer would have been different if you'd asked me while I was alive."

"Precisely. In life, you carry around so much guilt. Do you know why?"

"No, why?"

"It's because you don't know who you are in life. You don't understand that you are an eternal entity, with unlimited free will. Your senses of right and wrong are fictions made up by your man-made religions, government, laws, cultures and parents. And when you stray or go outside the lines drawn by these institutions, you feel guilty, don't you?"

"I definitely felt guilty. For most of my life I carried a huge feeling of guilt that became so intense it sometimes broke my spirit."

"You broke your own spirit by not realizing this. God is not here to punish you. When you love your children, you love them unconditionally, so no matter what they have done, they are still your children and you still love them. Do you think humans are capable of greater compassion than God? You do this, yet deny the hypocrisy."

"I had never thought about it that way but why do I feel so detached from my life as Jacob?"

"It was a lifetime ago and it was nothing more than a dream. Do you feel attachment or guilt or anger for a dream you had while living in the body as Jacob? You go to sleep, have dreams, and wake up, true?"

"Yes, that's correct."

"If you killed someone in a dream, did you feel as though you committed an unforgivable crime when you woke up?"

"No, it was just a dream."

"This is the vantage point from where you now currently see things. Life in the body is a short dream in the existence of your soul."

"Does this even take into account the most heinous of crimes on earth? What of genocide or murder, even rape, the hurting of innocents?"

"Yes, this does take those incidents into account. But before I answer, I will pose a question to you. Do you believe something can happen to God without him knowing or allowing it to happen?"

"I suppose not. How could anything happen to him which he would not allow to happen?"

"That's right, you're beginning to remember." She smiled at James and he could feel love radiate from it.

"So you're saying that all of those horrific crimes are accepted?"

"There must be a polar experience of love in order for love itself to exist. Those who decide to experience extreme acts of negativity are here to demonstrate what we are not so that we can better understand what we are. They have agreed to do so before entering the body, and it is their choice. If no one ever agreed to those experiences, then we would never have a negative reference point. We desire reference points to better understand that we are individuated aspects of God. Any choice away from those positive aspects will yield negative results. Cause and effect: the simple truth of the universe. Nothing more needs to be said."

"You said something before about man-made religions. Are all religions on Earth man-made?

"Do you believe God made them?"

"That's what we're told. I guess I don't understand what religions are."

Vivian explained that religions were essentially vehicles to pass what they called the Great Water, or the distance from ignorance to ultimate knowing. On one side of the Great Water was complete love, awaiting unification. On the other was every human in their own boat. Some people band together in larger boats and form common beliefs; these boats made up all religions. "This may help the soul experience certain realities relevant to that particular culture or theology."

"That can't be. I mean, how can all religions do the same thing if they often run into conflict with one another?"

"Well, because profit and power come into play. And because, at some level, most of these structured or organized belief systems propose that the afterlife is designed around some sort of punitive system of judgement. So, humans mimic this belief in law, business, personal relationships, and, on a grander scale, with religion as well. By judging others for their differences, they are, in fact, playing God by their own definitions."

"I don't understand. How does this help me stop Luzige?"

"Because without this clarity, you can't stop him. I tell you this to help remove your own judgements. When you understand that there are no victims and no villains, you will see the way."

"You mentioned my brother on Earth, the brother of Jacob. Why?"

"He will be instrumental in your fight against Luzige. You must protect him if your mission is to be successful."

"How is he instrumental when I don't even know him?"

"In life as Jacob, you did not know him, however in reality, he was working behind the scenes, watching you, and even helping you. He was the real source of the letters that were sent to you. He infiltrated the Arabe'en, and realized the role you'd play."

"Does he know he has a brother?" *Or am I just another face to him?*

"He was made aware through his work with the government. He wanted to help you, but couldn't reveal himself. But now, you must save him, as he is the only one with access to one of the last remaining Auditum Headsets you created."

"Save him from what?"

"Save him from those who will take revenge and make an example unto others. Above all, Luzige despises treachery and will torture and kill him to get the headset. You must move quickly."

"Thank you, Vivian. I know what I have to do next." James gave her a small smile which she returned. "Where will I find him?" he asked.

"He will be with the Arabe'en who remain, mounting a resistance. Find them in the city and they will help you. You two have a spiritual bond that cannot be broken, one that is stronger than you realize. But all in due time, my son. For now, I'll give you time to study alone in these majestic halls. Take this book." She handed him the large book she had been holding.

The book was beautifully engraved in some ancient lettering with gold trim. It was his life book, the book of Jacob. Detailing every account, every event which transpired in his life suddenly seemed very daunting. *Am I Jacob, James, or Lukman?* All he remembered was his experience as Jacob, a man still unsure of himself and lost in something so much bigger than he was. He remembered Tamara and his love for her as well.

"I sense your confusion," Vivian said. "Who you are right now is exactly who you need to be. There is nothing wrong with being who you are or being where you are in your process, for it is exactly as it is meant to be. You don't have to fear it because fear is the illusion.

"Thank you." James moved forward to hug her, and all at once he felt her love, protection, respect, and countless other aspects too complex to name or describe. "Thank you for spending time with me, and helping me," he whispered.

"Remember: I will be with you always. If you need me, you may call on me, for in this realm we are all things and in all places. We will never be separated again."

"What comes next?" James asked her.

"You may study here for as long as you like, and then you will be greeted by another. He is an old friend of yours, but I will say no more. You have much to discuss. Goodbye, my son."

"Goodbye, Mother"

And just as quickly as she appeared in his life, she was gone.

# SIX

## NOWHERE LAND

ALONE WITH HIS books and studies, James felt comfortable, like he always did when he read, even though what he held in his hand was more like an oracle than a book. The story of his life. He had loved, lost, wept, cheered, avenged, and died. He came to know more about himself through this book than he knew in life. He could see the patterns that emerged, the people that he had met, who they were, and how he had affected others.

The book literally portrayed a holographic image in his head, speeding through his life with crystal clarity, easily absorbed by his consciousness. James was at peace while he watched, as if he was watching a favourite movie. As with any movie, watching it a second time with different eyes allowed him to see things he had missed the first time. He moved through relationships in his life, seeing that they were there to either advance or hinder him. Vices were there to distract him from what would eventually become his destiny, a delay tactic before he did what was required. Negativity was also there to accentuate the times of love and peace. He looked back and saw the final moments of life with those he had loved. His father was there with him throughout all of his lives, and James hadn't even realized it. Orion had been his brother in past lives, his best friend, and even his son. In each life he had had, he'd never realized how much he'd been influenced by Orion. *How cliché, to only realize the worth of a person after they're gone.*

James saw the people that he had helped throughout his days on Earth, and the people they in turn helped through his example. There were also the people that he had rejected, and how that had added to their existing pain. He had never realized how each action could have a ripple effect like that. *If we saw the true consequences of each action we took, the world itself would change overnight.*

James found the details of his last few months as Jacob. He learned about the struggle with Aidan and Luzige. A duel in the astral realms weakened Aidan, allowing Luzige to possess him. He had entered Aidan's vessel in order to enter the physical realm and begin his reign of destruction upon Earth. James saw that he was the cause of many of the natural and unnatural disasters, feeding off human hatred and war.

James saw Tamara, the woman he had loved as Jacob, and still loved as James. She had gently guided him through this world, helping him to prepare and teaching him who he really was. She had led him to the lake of life, the multi-coloured waters that flowed through each person, strengthening their essence and connecting them with source energy. She had introduced him to Lucious and Boulos as well.

He remembered Tarif who was now lost within himself, trapped in the Abyss and unable to escape the bonds inflicted by his own beliefs. He had risked his life to tell Jacob that he had been identified by Netex from the beginning, and that he was being drugged with Catalyst and monitored by the government. Jacob had suspected the government was involved and somehow working with Aidan, but he couldn't prove it. That would ensure Inspector Moretti had sufficient evidence against Edward Aidan and his illegal human trials of the Catalyst. Tarif died trying to get James that information, and he wouldn't let him suffer for it. *Hold on my friend, I'm coming to get you.*

James felt a burst of energy that suddenly transported him to another dimension. As he shifted, a symbol flashed through his mind. He relaxed, assuming it was part of his education. But he sensed the remnants of a dark energy in this. *Who brought me here?*

He looked around to see mountains that looked like blue energy, shimmering in the distance against a sky painted with an array of pink, light blue, and shimmering white as dusk settled in. The clouds were a deep purple, moving only slightly to reveal the vast mountainous landscape in the distance. He wore a tattered cloak which sheltered him against the wind while he walked towards arches. They were tendrils of white and blue energy flowing through a large mystical structure. He pushed on toward a blue castle spire made out of steel and stone. It looked like an abandoned watch tower from a time long since forgotten. There was a light in one of the upper windows, so he pressed on to find someone else to speak with, and perhaps figure out where he was.

The door to the spire seemed sturdy, and made of wood. It contained a single door knocker and nothing else. James wondered how a single knocker could alert anyone in this dimension, where the winds seemed to be eternally raging. He raised the knocker and slammed it three times, which, to his surprise, echoed throughout the spire. The wind around him became stronger, and he could hear the chirping of birds approaching. He looked about to see where the noise came from, but saw clouds of darkness approaching, moving about rapidly. They overtook the Blue Mountains, and swept down the country side. Faster and faster they approached, and he realized the chirping came from these clouds of darkness. They were not flocks of birds at all, but some sort of vicious bats. James could see them sweeping past the spire at a rapid pace as they travelled in packs, emitting a type of dark smoke as they flapped their wings. They began circling the spire as he slammed the knocker down several more times, hoping to get inside. The spire soon had these bat-like entities swirling around it, as the first one came in for a gash across his face. James recoiled as the next one came and attacked, then two and three. They were striking him with a vicious force that felt like he'd just been sliced. He knocked more furiously, but no one answered.

He figured this to be the end as the flocks of these monsters overtook him, until the spire door suddenly opened, and a hand grabbed him and pulled him inside, the door slamming quickly behind them. It was warm inside; he felt a breath of relief invigorate him as he opened his eyes to gaze upon the person who saved his life. She stood about 5'5" tall, wearing a cloak over a modest set of pants, white shirt, and hiking boots. The cloak did not reveal her face, but James could tell by her form that she was female. "Thank you for saving me from those things."

"Those were the Nephiliers. They scour the lands here at night, seeking any living thing they can feed on."

"Wow, I was lucky to find you."

"Lucky indeed. My spire is the only structure for a great distance. A few have made it here, but most have perished. What brings you here, traveler?" She walked towards a nearby table which had a rather large hunting knife on top, a lamp, and a map. She rested her hand near the knife.

"My name is James. I'm looking for some friends. I believe they are trapped in one of these lower realms, and I'm looking for a guide." He eyed her hand resting near the knife in case she decided to use it against him.

"Hah, you are looking for your friends and you need a guide? Do you have any idea how many dimensions there are?"

"No, I assume there are many, which is why I need help finding them."

"Dear James, you must be joking. There are infinite dimensions, infinite times within dimensions, and even more ways to hide. No one can help you find your friends." She chuckled, a light feminine sound.

"No, no, that can't be. I was told this was what had to be done."

"By whom?" James still couldn't see her face, but he felt her stare at him from beneath her darkened cowl.

"A monk named Lucious. He told me to come here; this is supposed to be the entrance to the Abyss. This is where they are, my friends. Lucious told me so."

"He lied." She took down her cowl, revealing her red hair, beautiful face and dark eyes. "This is not the entrance to the Abyss. This is Nowhere Land."

Nowhere Land was a place between the folds of the prime dimensions. It was the only place that people were free from consequence. It also had no entrance, or exit. It was overrun by demons and nomads.

"What do you mean no entrance or exit to this place?"

"I mean whoever told you to come here has tricked you. The only people who know of this place are the Jinn, those they have trapped, and those who work for them. You can only find this place by falling through one of the cracks in reality, or by willing yourself here. There is no entrance to this place, you simply arrive here, like you did. And I'm afraid, there is no exit either." She rolled her eyes and sighed, flipping her red hair back over her shoulder from where it had fallen over her face. "Why did he tell you to come here?"

"He told me that in order to end the torment of Luzige, I had to free my friends and mount an attack. When I was transported here, I saw a symbol in my mind. I also felt a dark energy surrounding me. He told me that I had to rescue my friends in the lower realms. The realm where Luzige holds his victims captive. He told me to come here!"

"Do you remember the symbol? Can you draw it?" She seemed almost intrigued now.

"Hmm, it was complex but maybe I can, or I can try. Who are you?"

"I'm Shyla; I am a JuKari, a Way Seer. This is my home; I live here in this tower."

"You live here, in Nowhere Land? How did you get here?"

"I fell through one of the cracks in reality that I told you about. There are dimensions within deep space which have 'Feeders.' These are holes in the universe that suck in matter and energy for consumption by this dimension. It feeds the universe what it needs to sustain itself. These Feeders are like holes that are punched in the universe, and are literally rifts between realities themselves. I was travelling with friends when we spotted some Draconians and attempted to flee. We flew too close to the Feeder and we were pulled in. The next moment I was here." She shrugged.

"Where did your friends go? Who are the Draconians?"

"Draconians are a reptile like species; they are warriors from the fifth dimension. They are not to be trifled with. Some of them were also sucked into the Feeder, some ended up here, and I guess some ended up on the other side of the Feeder, wherever that is. My friends suffered the same fate, I'm afraid. This happened a long time ago, and most have perished. Others attempted to find an exit from this place, but I found shelter here."

"How do you know that they haven't escaped?"

"Don't you understand? No one escapes this place. You either survive or die."

"Wait a minute. I thought I couldn't die in these other dimensions. I thought dying was only a mortal circumstance, something associated with a physical body. How is it I can die here as well?"

"Oh, there is death here, except this death will wipe you out of existence itself. When you die here, you are erased from creation. Like you never existed at all. I am going to rest and I suggest you do the same. There is a chesterfield in the back room. When morning comes, you need to leave. Good night."

Shyla went upstairs and took an oil lamp to light the way. She looked human, but James could never tell when it came to other worlds, so he took nothing for granted. She said she was a JuKari. That must be some other humanoid civilization, perhaps with origins in upper dimensions. Earth was still in the third dimension, one of the most dense and prone to darkness. Vibrations were what determined dimension, and because humans collectively resonated at such a low vibration, a low frequency, they were limited in their perceptions of the third dimension. It had been said that with higher thoughts, words, and actions, humans could collectively raise their vibrations to higher realms, but James wasn't sure.

He barely slept through the night, not even sure what sleep meant in these other worlds. Nevertheless, he was rejuvenated, much like sleep on Earth. Dreams took on a life of their own in these worlds, creating realities more vivid than he ever thought possible. James thought of his physical self, lying there, vulnerable. It was a sickening feeling to be at the mercy of this dimension, unable to awake from a dream. But one thing he did realize was that these journeys seemed to bend time, so that barely a few moments passed in physical life. He hoped that was the case with this journey.

A red and purple sun began to rise amid the shimmering mountains. This place seemed to be created by pure energy, but only half created, thus revealing the very essence of light which formed its landscape. Everything was alive and everything moved.

"Beautiful, isn't it?" Shyla walked behind James as he stared out the window.

He jumped at the sound of her voice and spun around to face her. "Yes it is," he said.

"Hard to believe it can be so dangerous here. The mountains are host to several monsters of consciousness. Many of them arrived here, but most have been sent here by the Jinn. When creations of theirs get out of control, they usually dispose of them by sending them here, to the folds between dimensions. Let me ask you, James: this monk of yours, what did he look like?"

"Lucious? He wore a robe, gray and tattered. He tied it with a modest yellowish rope around his waist. He wore a straw hat as well."

"Those are the common garbs of a Shaytaan. He is a demon who works for the Jinn. He tricked you, I'm afraid."

"No, that cannot be. Lucious saved me and my friends, he is helping us defeat Luzige. He's on our side."

"Is he now? Do you not know where he has sent you? As I said before, there is no escape from this place, James. You are trapped. Forget about any other life you once had, because this is it. You cannot manifest, you cannot create, and you cannot affect reality in the slightest way. You cannot shift or travel away from this place; your thoughts are useless here. This is worse than the Abyss, because your only options are to survive and become a nomad like me or else be devoured into nothingness."

"How can you give up like this?"

"James, I have been here long enough to see the sun rise and fall hundreds of thousands of times. I have been here longer than I can remember."

"But what kind of existence is this anyway? Cowering in a tower like this, hiding from monsters in the night. How can you not even try to escape? There is always a way. There must be a way!"

"Come, let me show you something." She led him down a corridor made of stones forged by someone long ago. She lit the way with her lamp, as there was no electricity or power of any sort running through the structure. James wondered where she got her oil, and thought perhaps it was powered by something else entirely. They approached a staircase and she walked deliberately down the steps. "Almost there."

"Where are you taking me?"

"I have fashioned a workshop in the basement. I'd like to show you what I've been working on all this time." She continued down the hall which revealed a large wooden door at the end. There was light underneath, coming from inside the room. She took out a set of keys from her pocket, and opened the lock. A large metallic clicking noise could be heard as the doors creaked open. The room was covered in maps. Maps of all sizes and kinds, which seemed to draw out the landscape of what I could only assume was Nowhere Land.

"What is all this?"

"This is Nowhere Land. In ancient times, there were those in your world who believed the world was flat, and that you could fall off the face of the planet itself. Well, here the edge of the world brings you right back to the other side. As you walk away, you are brought back from whence you came. There is no exit. It took me years to realize what was happening. It was only until I found the same tower we are in right now that I understood. Over and over again I walked, and I kept seeing the same tower. The edge of the road is the beginning of the very same street that leads back here. There is no escape." She paused, and looked down at the ground, off to the left, obviously deep in thought.

"Unless your symbol has something to do with this. Over here, there's an empty canvas and some coal that you can use to draw the symbol.

"When I talked to Lucious, he told me that this symbol has many meanings." James started to draw the outer circle.

"When you asked me how I got here, I thought the symbol had something to do with it…" From what he recalled, the inside had a slight cross in the centre, but it curved off at the top. "Lucious said my mission would make me whole again, that I'm somehow fragmented. I don't know who I am, but maybe this could help."

He couldn't stop drawing the symbol and it was as if another force was taking control, finishing the symbol for him.

"The symbol has great power but I'm not sure how it's used," Shyla said. She stood up quickly, realizing something that made her face twist into an expression of fear. "I've seen it only one other time, on the wall of the Scorpion's lair. I've stumbled into there only once, on one of my expeditions across this world. Somehow that Scorpion has the key to get out of here. He's the gate keeper. I didn't leave unharmed." She turned away from him and loosened her garb, revealing her beautiful back but further down there was an enormous scar across her torso where it looked like she was nearly torn apart.

"Did that thing do this to you?"

"Yes. It saw me and looked right at me. It's enormous. My first instinct was to run, but it was too fast. I guess it took pity on me, as it only sliced me from behind, sending me hurling down the mountain face. I've seen it do worse."

"I'm sorry you had to go through that, but we need to get out of here. I can't stay here and neither can you. How big is Nowhere Land?"

"Here, look at the map. We're right here." She adjusted her clothing, and pointed to a rather large map with a tower as the main focal point. There seemed to be some other structures to the north, mostly mountains, and a lake. There were markings along the edges of the map.

"What are these here, these markings at the edge?"

"Those are the streets which lead to nowhere. They lead you right back to where you started. I believe this one at the North West edge of the map brings you right back to the southeast path over here. Like I said, there's no way out of here."

"I'm not ready to believe that, Shyla. Over here, what are those ruins on this big map?"

"That's the inner cloister, the closest thing there is to a city around here. People there huddle together for protection and survival."

"Protection from what? You said before that this place is some sort of wasteland for creatures. What did you mean by that?"

"I mean that there is existence and non-existence. Non-existence is not simply an area of nothingness, it is full of creations which will never exist. Monstrosities of the imagination. During the times of creation's earliest days of being, there were experiments of creation which served no real purpose other than to destroy. These ancient relics were cast into non-existence, a dimension of suspended animation. Some of those monsters fell through the cracks and ended up here in Nowhere Land. The Scorpion is one of those monsters. He's also known as the Soul Collector."

"Some of those monsters ended up here? How?"

"Some of the Jinn have been around since the earliest days of the creation. They are some of the oldest entities among us, some of the wisest and most powerful as well. They can also be some of the most vengeful creatures in existence. Some Jinn witnessed the creation of these strange monsters and can even remember their names. Much of this information has been lost, but once it is found, a Jinn can call forth a creature from the prison of non-existence and conjure them back into our reality."

"Why? What purpose would that serve?"

"Complete and total destruction. But once called forth, it is not so easy to banish a creature back to non-existence. But where else can you put such a monster? Well, they found a place. Right here."

"So what are we up against?"

"Up against? There is no stopping these things, there is no confronting them. I have only seen two of these monsters, as they mostly lie dormant. But what I saw was horrific. They can walk through a town completely unhindered, destroying everything. They blast through waves of people, turning them to dust. If you see one, you run."

# SEVEN

## LEVIATHAN

I T WAS AWHILE later that James had convinced Shyla to bring him to the city. He wanted to meet other entities who had settled in this land long since forgotten. During the day, the land looked much like a barren desert wasteland, with a few deadened trees and hills scattered about. Shyla seemed to know the way despite the fact that much of it looked the same. They soon came upon a city made from rubble and stone. A market was visible near the centre square where there was rustling and people talking. Some men could be seen setting up tents and tables, while women and children were busying themselves with customers. Some form of bartering was occurring with no visible form of money.

"Shyla, where did all these people come from? There must be at least a few thousand people in this city."

"I told you, the rifts. People have gathered here over hundreds of years, and have somehow managed to get along…for the most part."

"And these rifts, when do they occur? If people come through, maybe we can leave the same way."

"I thought of that already. The problem is that these rifts open randomly just like how you got here. Predicting a time and place is next to impossible."

*Maybe Shyla is right,* he thought. "Where are we going?"

"I'm taking you to see a friend; he might be able to help."

"How can he help?"

"He's been here the longest, so maybe he knows something."

They walked onwards through the market. At one of the stalls, there were a number of short, old ladies wearing tattered clothes with several metal bobbles on a table in front of them. James slowed his pace to look at the trinkets. Many pieces were fashioned into rings or charms with engravings on them, but the symbols were foreign to him.

Other tables had necklaces and bracelets carved from glowing stones. They shone brilliant colours, primarily a dark green or blue. "What are these made of?" James asked a young boy who ran one of necklace stands and he pointed to the mountains behind us.

"It's made from the mountain rock. It's very special; it keeps you safe. Buy one!"

"I'm afraid I don't have anything to give you, I'm sorry."

"What about that necklace you're wearing, it's pretty nice." *What necklace?* He reached into his shirt, and realized he was wearing a gold necklace with a tear drop amulet. *Where did this come from?*

"Come, James, we should go. Forget about the necklace." Shyla grabbed him by the arm and pulled him away from the boy.

"Hey, come on, lady, I was going to make a trade!" The boy shouted as they walked away. James could see a swarm of bats start to rise in the distance.

"Not too much further. I want to be out of here before sundown." She seemed very nervous, which put James on alert.

Shyla wore a vest of leather armour, contoured around her feminine core. Her midriff was showing enough to reveal her belly button, and her pants were held up by a belt which had her hunting knife attached. A satchel over her left shoulder sank down to her hip. This was nearly covered by her red cloak, buttoned by an unusual golden seal near her neck.

"There clearly seems to be some dangerous people here," James remarked. Many dangerous men were about, with dark shrouded clothing, only their eyes visible. James could also see the metallic glimmer of various forms of weaponry. Axes, maces and swords. They were scattered about the city, like vultures looking for prey. "Yes, there are many thieves and killers here," She said. "They have already spotted you. We need to move quickly. They know you're new here."

"What do they want?"

"Whatever they can find." She walked through a crowded bank of people, and James struggled to keep up. He could hear the bats shrieking behind him.

"Hurry!" She seemed to be making her way towards a large closing gate, a massive group of people attempting to get in. People were shouting and jostling for position. Five large men guarded the entrance, selecting the people who could enter.

"What going on, Shyla?"

"Try to keep up! They're going to close the gate, and my friend is inside. If we don't get in there, we have to find shelter for the night." Time was of the essence and he pushed his way closer to her. He was almost behind her when she started talking to one of the guards.

"Okay, Shyla, come in." His voice was slow and bear-like. All of the guards resembled some form of ancient executioner.

"He's with me."

"Alright. Get in, hurry." They both squeezed in as the gate closed. People could be heard screaming and complaining. They quickly started to disperse, realizing the doors wouldn't be opening again anytime soon.

"What was that all about?" James asked.

"We came from the market outside the city gates. We're now inside the city. Many people live inside the city but most of the vendors don't. They try to get in from time to time, but they aren't allowed. They start packing up when the gates close otherwise they won't last until morning."

"What happens to them?"

"They're devoured."

That had not been the answer James was expecting, but it didn't shock him either. "By what?"

"Come on, let's find my friend."

"You haven't answered my question!" James hated it when people shrugged off his questions.

"The darkness devours people. Just like it almost took you."

"I thought those were just bats."

"That's one of its forms, yes." She began walking down the street and he followed behind her. The city was large, with cobblestone streets and buildings of modest architecture were about. It was definitely a city that had been there for quite some time. In James's opinion, the people had built it up quite nicely with spires and a town square visible from where they stood.

"What is your friend's name?"

"Does it matter?" She asked sharply.

"I guess not. How can he help us?"

"His name is KKormak. I've told you, there's no way out of this place."

"Yes, and?"

"Maybe there's a way in."

"What the hell are you talking about?"

"It's just something someone once said to me. Maybe there's another way to look at the problem. You asked for help, James, and this is the best I've got."

"I appreciate everything you've done." James remained silent for a while as they walked towards KKormak's home. The sun began to set, and she assured him they'd be there shortly. People were packing up their chairs and tables, bringing them inside. Windows were closed and barred up, doors could be heard locking. People were certainly protecting themselves from the darkness they feared so much.

"It's just through this alley way." She took him through a tight passageway between two buildings. Our path revealed a modest door attached to a small square structure, presumably his home.

Shyla knocked on the door a few times. Nothing. She tried once again. The door opened showing a dark, dimly lit room but there was no one visible.

"Come on, let's go." She walked in, and James followed. In the corner there stood a large grandfather clock next to a lamp resting on a table. Nothing else could be heard but the ticking clock.

"Shyla. To what do I owe the pleasure of your company? And look, you've brought a friend." From across the room, in pure darkness, sat a barely visible man. His voice was snake-like, deep and rough.

"KKormak, I've brought a friend named James. He comes from the physical world. He's not like us."

"Oh, I think he's very much like us. I think he's trapped and needs a way home. Just. Like. Us. Isn't he?"

"Yes, and I thought—"

"I know what you thought. You thought that since I'm the oldest, one of the first ones, that maybe I'd know something, right? Maybe there would be some magical way, or some secret door to get out."

"Something like that."

"There is no doorway out of this place, little girl, you know that. The only way out of here is by destruction. When you are devoured, you are certainly not here anymore, are you? You're gone. The Soul Collector makes sure of that."

"What is that?" James asked.

"It's the ancient Leviathan. The destroyer of souls your physical world seems to colour so brilliantly in your books. He resides in this realm along with many other interesting entities of creation."

"What do you mean?" James probed further.

"There are many demons here that are your nightmares. Many that have haunted dreams and tortured souls."

"Where are these things?"

"They live in the mountains and only come out at night. The Scorpions."

James sighed. *It really is hopeless, then.* "Come on, Shyla, this guy can't help us." He motioned towards the door and began to walk out.

"Thank you KKormak. I just thought..." Shyla trailed off and began to follow James out the door.

"Wait, come back." They stopped and turned around.

"There might be a way. Only might be. But it's impossible, you see, that's why I say there is no way out of here."

"Tell me!" James shouted. "I was betrayed by a monk. That's why I'm here. I have a physical body waiting for me. I have to get out of this place and get back to my life!"

"What an interesting statement. Do you not consider this life? This is all I know, little man. This is all I've ever been. But I understand. You've visited our world through your dreams, and now you've trapped yourself in a place that's a little more real than you imagined possible."

"I never believed this could happen. How can my mind be trapped here when I have a body that needs food, air, water, and sleep?"

"Ah yes, sleep. Something we do so often in physical life, but give such little attention. The mind is the power tool of creation." KKormak smiled, and told James that the mind kept creating in sleep, like it did when it was awake. It allowed a person to find a perspective to use for interacting and functioning, creating that person's reality. But if a person's mind is trapped in another world, then they can go mad. Their physical body would start showing it, as if they were hallucinating. Or they could be comatose.

"Are you telling me that I'm fighting for my sanity here?" James asked. "For my very life in the physical world?"

"No, son. You're fighting for your very existence." He spoke calmly, as if the answer was simple.

"What about you, where did you come from? Don't you have a body waiting for you somewhere?"

"Oh, I imagined I had a body once long ago. In fact, I vaguely remember having another life. But it was so long ago. I'm sure that if I ever had a body, its essence had turned to dust. Yet here I am, still living in this hell hole."

"Please, KKormak, I have a life to get back to. Help us." He rarely begged or pleaded, but it was necessary this time.

"Very well. I will tell you what I know. The world you see around you is not how it always was. This world here, this island of nothingness was created by the Architects, beings trusted to construct certain realms."

The Architects needed a dividing line, or a reality between realities, to keep other realities from bleeding into each other. The reality they were in was only supposed to act as a buffer, so the dimensional reality was very limited. "There are several of these realms of nothingness throughout creation," KKormack said. "And in this particular realm, this place I affectionately call 'Nowhere Land,' I was the first humanoid to enter. The darkness was already here when I arrived, along with those monsters."

"How did you get here?"

"Oh, I was banished by a creature not unlike your monk, I imagine. Differently from you, I've never taken on physical bodies, or none that I recall. I have no interest in that, so I cannot relate to your sense of urgency. You see, I have been here for many thousands of years, but I don't know for certain because I've stopped counting. How I got here had a lot to do with the choices I had made, or failed to make. I had always preferred taking my own path, but I had started hanging out with the wrong crowd, if you catch my drift."

"I see. Tell me, KKormak, how do I get out of here?"

"You must confront the Soul Collector, the Scorpion."

"But that's impossible!" Shyla shouted. Just then, the gentle rumbling James had heard became more audible and rough. He could hear things moving outside, slowly getting closer to them. Black streaks flew by and he quickly shut the door before pulling down the large wooden arm which barred it closed. KKormak turned up the lamp which lit most of the room. There appeared to be a hallway leading to a larger back half of the complex.

"Smart move." KKormak moved across the room. He got up and moved towards the lamp, revealing his face. He wore a leather mask with straps covering most of his face, but James could tell it was oddly shaped, as if he had been deformed. His mouth was large, as was his nose. His hair was dark and stringy; he stood rather large, well over six feet tall. His frame was surprisingly strong and muscled. He wore a dark, sleeveless vest that covered some type of black chain-mail.

"KKormak, how can you tell him to fight the Collector?" Shyla asked. "Nothing can stop it."

"When I came here, Shyla, there was nothing but vast oceans of energy and some mass, but nothing really here. After I attempted and failed to escape, I tried to shape the energy into something but could not. I was truly in a wasteland. But that all changed when the skies ripped open, revealing the eye of something ancient staring down. A giant eye looked through the tear in the sky, and suddenly the Collector was thrown into this world. It landed in the pool of energy, and then the sky closed up. The Collector somehow forged this land out of the energies. It shot power out of its mouth, claws, and tail, forming the realm as you see it. It formed rocks and mountains and eventually created its home deep beneath the stone. Over time, more people began to appear. Many had stories about falling between cracks in some sub-reality and ending up here. There are maybe a thousand of us, I'm not sure. Human life anyway, I'm talking about. There are other entities of darkness which have shown up as well, which is why we lock the doors at night. But only this creature had the power to form the mountains, perhaps it also has the power to open a rift out of here."

"So what are we up against?" James asked in earnest.

"It unleashes a stream of energy that devours and consumes you until there is nothing left. Before the walls were built, it came many times, feasting on the people of this city."

"Then how can we stop it?"

"It may be monstrous, but it may not be completely invincible. Above the mouth, where its energy streams from, there are eyes, many of them. I'm guessing if you can somehow get on top of it and stab its eyes, there may be a shot at killing it."

"Maybe a shot? Wouldn't I be vulnerable to its claws and tail while resting on its head?"

"Yes."

"Then I don't understand."

"The energy this ancient monster uses is primal, or elemental. It is the energy of creation itself. How else could it form the mountains of this reality? When it consumes you, it somehow replenishes its power and then lies dormant for a time. If you can somehow absorb this power, you may be able to form more than just landscape. You may be able to fashion a doorway into another dimension: a way out."

"And how am I supposed to accomplish this? I'm only a man."

"Are you? There was something about you from the moment I saw you, something different. Shyla sees it too, otherwise she wouldn't have brought you here. Isn't that right, Shyla?"

She nodded her head, as she walked over to the table, revealing more maps from her satchel. "I saw it in you the moment you came knocking on my door. There was no need for you to hide from those creatures, was there?"

"No, I suspect not. I think our friend here is special. Aren't you, James?" KKormak suddenly walked towards him, grabbing him by the throat, and lifting him off the ground using only one arm. His arms and chest were massive, and James could feel him choking the life out of him.

"What...are you...doing?"

"Come on, just a little longer." He tightened his grip and smiled. James could feel extreme pressure in his head. He was about to black out when he instinctively grabbed KKormak's hand and pulled back his finger, twisting it fiercely. James could see him loosen his grip. KKormak moved forward, giving James the range he needed to launch a couple stinging blows to his forehead and nose. He dropped him, stumbling backwards a few steps, as James moved in, unleashing several strikes to his ribs, jaw and neck. A flurry of strikes followed as he tried to get up, but KKormak was unable to match James's speed or targeting. He finished him with an elbow strike to his back, and KKormak collapsed on the ground, his massive frame now anything but a challenge.

James disengaged and looked around. Shyla sat and stared at him, her mouth wide open. She shook her head slowly back and forth. "How did you do that? You toppled KKormak so easily; someone with his strength should have quickly killed you."

"Perhaps killing me is not as easy as you think."

"I guess not."

# PART II

## ANTI-MATTER

*"There is still time, traveler. Your brother Joshua is being held captive in the city, in a large tower controlled by Luzige. Rescue him because he has the device you created on earth: Auditum. Use this to find your friends in the other world, for they will know what you must do."*

# EIGHT

"**B**RAVO. BRAVO." A stumbling KKormak said as he clapped and struggled to regain his balance. James helped him up. "Just as I thought, you are special. I figured I'd have to squeeze it out of you. Who taught you how to fight like that?"

"I don't know. Instinct, I guess."

"James, when you were in the middle of striking KKormak, you began to glow white. Did you notice?" Shyla asked.

"No, I didn't."

"Yes, you began shimmering with a white light as your velocity increased. It was as if you were turning into something else. Then, when you stopped hitting him, you stopped glowing. I've never seen anything like it."

KKormak grabbed his ribs, and walked to the chair near her. "I saw it too. And I've only ever seen that once before, when I worked for the Jinn. Luzige had me attack a group of elders from the higher realms once. I was supposed to stop them from creating something powerful, something important. I moved in to see what they were doing, and they were working on a body. Then, one of the elders turned to me. They all wore robes hiding their faces, but when one turned to me, he began to glow like you. Then the next thing I remember, I was on the ground. The Jinn was not pleased with my performance, and I was trapped here. James, you shine like that elder did."

"What does that mean?"

"For now, it means you can fight really well. And you might be the only chance we have at getting out of here. You might not understand it, but you have to trust it. That's all I know."

"Alright."

Shyla was already looking through her maps. She rifled around in her bag, looking for something specific.

"Here it is, the Collector's home. We can find it deep in the mountains, beyond the black corpus. That area is covered by assassins, like those you saw in the streets. There is other wild astral life in the area as well: wolves, bats, tigers. It's very dangerous."

"Is that the only way to get to the creature?"

"It's the only way I know of. I have never gone there myself, but when I saw the Collector many years ago, that's the direction it headed."

"I think we need to rest now, or at least I certainly do. Tomorrow I'll show you my armoury, and you can gather what you need for your journey. Good night." KKormak walked down the hallway, towards his bedroom. "There are rooms upstairs. Shyla will show you."

"Let's go. I'll show you where you can rest." She walked upstairs ahead of James.

"So, James, what is making love like in your world? The place you came from." She asked while brushing her hair from her face.

"I wouldn't know. It's not something I've had the opportunity to experience, not that I can remember anyway."

"You don't remember anything at all?"

"I've had dreams, and glimpses of things from another time, but that's all."

"I wonder, have you ever made love in other dimensions?"

"Umm, not that I remember."

"Come, your room's just over here." She walked into a modest room with a bed and a night stand with a lamp. She sat on the bed, taking off her elbow and shoulder armour, dropping them to the floor, revealing her soft and delicate outline.

"I'm thinking, James, tonight might be my last night in existence. If the Collector catches me or you, we will be destroyed, or worse yet, erased from creation. But I'm okay with that, because surviving here is not much of a life anyway. What I'm trying to say is will you sleep with me tonight, James?" She let down her red hair, swaying it from side to side, enticing him. He had not had any form of physical interaction at all while living as James, and she was beautiful.

What followed was something unlike earthly love-making. James had found a magazine once in George's garage, which quickly reminded him of the base yet arousing mechanics of love making, but this was nothing like that. Between them glowed a warm brilliant light that began to pulse and rage, growing and all-consuming. A bright light enveloped them as they moved in towards each other and their lips touched for the first time. The feeling was a magnificent merger of their essences, and in the moments that followed, the most exquisite feeling washed over James as they came to realize who they truly were. Through energetically becoming one, he saw and felt many of her life experiences, and many aspects of her identity. Her vulnerabilities and strengths, her triumphs and traumas were all revealed. Yet he sensed that the greatest truth of her personality was kept from him. This is what she called making love.

The morning brought haste and foreboding. KKormak brought James into his armory, opening several large chests full of various hacking instruments. On the wall were crossbows, swords, axes, and shields. In the corner was a short metal staff. James walked over to it and picked it up. It had a button that caused the ends to snap out, revealing a larger staff approximately 5 feet in length. He liked it and decided to keep it. There were also some iron knuckles with large arching blades fashioned to the end. He took those along with a double sword set in a single sheath and was ready to go.

Shyla gathered some bows and arrows along with some knives,

which James presumed were for close quarter combat. A short while later, after assembling their weapons cache they thanked KKormak and left. It was his choice to stay, but he didn't have a body and life waiting for him like James did.

"Shyla, from what I gather, when the sun goes down here, and dark entities sweep the streets. That much I understand, but why do they not enter homes which are barred closed? Couldn't they just as easily crash through if they are so powerful?"

"Yes, they could. Except they are creatures of consciousness and they cannot cross the threshold of our homes without being invited. That is like entering our very minds. A creature of consciousness needs permission to do such things. But when we're out in the open, there is no convenient symbol like a door closing to help keep out the negative thoughts. They are able to surround us when we're out in the open, so they overtake us and feed on our fear. If they get a hold of you, you aren't the same after. That is, if you survive the encounter."

"And during the day, they aren't able to attack? Why is that?"

"I don't know; it has something to do with the light. They don't come out in the light."

"Have you ever been taken by them?" James wondered how she knew so much.

"I came very close. I could feel the darkness seeping inside. It was vicious, angry, and cold. The darkness tried to take me, but I saw the house I currently live in. I ran towards it, got inside and slammed the door shut. I've lived there ever since." They walked towards the rising sun and the East Mountains, where James originally saw the darkness spilling towards the lower plains. They walked for what seemed like hours, far away from the city, away from any doors or covering of any kind.

"How far are we supposed to walk, Shyla?"

"It'll take another couple of hours before we reach the mountain base. There's a walkway there which might cause us some trouble if we don't hurry up. We need to get through there before the sun sets."

"Why? What's through that pass?"

"That's the black corpus, the grounds where the assassins live. Some who have been taken by the darkness have joined it. They are scavengers and murders. They will be waiting for the sunset to take us, and they probably already know we're coming. Those shrouded men you saw in the city cloister, those were some."

"Alright, let's move faster then." They picked up the pace, reaching it in about an hour and a half. They were quicker than they could have been, but maybe not quick enough. They reached the passage way leading straight through the black corpus. The sun was resting low in the late afternoon sky.

"How long will it take to get through here?

"Well, if we make it all the way through, maybe about an hour or so."

"When does the sun go down?"

"In about an hour. Let's move. There are some caves near the top of the passage that might keep us safe for the night if we can block the entrance." They moved through the rocky passage, the trail worn and beaten down by human treading. The passage looked like it had been here for a hundred years at least, or perhaps longer. Trees of flowing dark blue light were seen on occasion, but what they mostly saw was dark rock. The mountain looked like energy from a distance, but was actually solid matter when seen from nearby. As they progressed, James got the feeling that they weren't alone. He could feel eyes peering at them from deep within the mountain crevices.

"Do you feel that?" He asked.

"Yes, I do. I don't think we're going to make it. The caves are about a 20 minute walk straight up from here, and the sun's going down in about five minutes. I can hear them now, jostling in the dark. They can barely contain themselves."

"I hear them too." James readied his staff, and got into position with plenty of room to move around, his back towards Shyla.

"We have to keep moving, whatever we do, we have to get to those caves. They can keep this up all night but we can't."

"Okay, let's move slowly; be aware of your surroundings."

"Here they come!" Shyla shouted.

"I see them! Ready your weapons!" Shyla began shooting into the darkness, which bled out from the mountain veins. The sun rolled out of sight, and darkness came, bringing with it waves of savages. Their faces were dark, with jagged teeth, horrid shaped eyes, and venomous glares. They wore black garments, cloaks, and coverings. Some had knives, others axes, still others with swords or makeshift clubs.

"Here they come!" James shouted. He began to tense up, assuming a fighting pose, hoping his combat skills would kick in, and they did. All at once, his skin glimmered with sparkling white light as he struck wave after wave of them. Spinning the staff, striking in rhythmic fashion, James cleared a circle around him and Shyla, beating anything that walked within distance. Shyla continuously shot her bow as they moved up the mountain path. Their hisses could be heard, as they tested the boundaries of James's perimeter. As they walked in, James took them out with ease.

Suddenly a group of orcs swarmed Shyla, but James jumped towards her, shielding her from the onslaught. He attacked them with crushing force, bones and faces breaking with each strike as he took out combatant after combatant. The pattern was repeated until they fired back with arrows of their own, hitting Shyla in the shoulder.

She yelled out as she fell to the ground.

"Are you okay?" James asked as he helped her up. She pulled the arrow out of her shoulder and valiantly continued shooting. James realized that there was no way they could continue. "We can't keep fighting them off! I don't know what else to do!"

"We're not going to make it. I'm sorry. We tried our best." Shyla began to buckle as she ran out of arrows, grabbing the knives from her belt as a last resort. The orcs had closed in, and there were too many of them for James and Shyla to fight. "Good bye, James. I'm sorry." James looked at Shyla down on one knee, thrashing at every enemy he touched, but he knew it was not enough. James couldn't fight them all. The darkness was vast; James could see it in waves behind each fighter he overtook. He thought of his life as James, his friends George, Jess, and his dreams of Tamara. The love that he knew he might never know again. *No, I won't go out like this. There has to be a way to stop them.*

Suddenly, there was a light and force emitted from James's body, knocking back all of their adversaries. They cowered and took shelter, fearing the light. James's body stayed in this state as he continued to emit pure energy, and his skin became sparkling white light. He turned towards Shyla and grabbed her into his arms, flying into the air with an enormous leap, towards the caves that were more than one thousand feet from where they had been.

Just then his skin returned back to normal and Shyla fell to the cave floor. James grabbed her to stop the fall. "What happened back there? You saved us! Even my shoulder, look at it: it's healed. What happened, what did you do?" Her questions came fast, her face pale. James thought she might be in shock.

James shrugged. "It was just instinct. Let's get inside, find shelter and rest for the night." She agreed as they made their way into the caves. There were large rocks near the cave entrance which were easily moved, blocking the way in and keeping the creatures out.

"There's something you're not telling me," Shyla said. "You just summoned some unknown force which destroyed everything back there, or at least sent those things running away. It was amazing, don't get me wrong, but what else aren't you saying?"

James sighed. "Do you remember that I told you I was sent here by Lucious? Well, he must have done it on purpose. He knows things about me that he wouldn't share. He invited me to his study and showed me a book, but was elusive and avoided answering my questions. Lucious said I'm some form of entity called a Galanic that breaks into three parts, a fragmented soul whose consciousness takes on different characteristics. From what I understand I underwent a voluntary process to break my psyche into different parts. This somehow resulted in different personas, of which I am one of them. The first identity was known as Jacob, and he… I died. Now I'm back, and now I'm here as James."

"So what's different about you this time?" Shyla asked, as she settled onto a flat rock.

"I guess we just found out how I'm different didn't we? I haven't quite figured all that out yet."

"So you're clearly super powered... but wait." Shyla looked concerned.

"Does that mean you're going to die too?" She asked genuinely scared.

"I hope not. But I don't know. What I understand about these three parts, is that there is always a piece of me connected... directly connected to the astral realm, or non-physical realms."

"But to serve what purpose?"

"Well, a safety net perhaps? I'm not so easily trapped in any one particular dimension that seems to be one advantage. And perhaps it also helped me materialize on earth as well. Orion, a friend I met in the Summerlands, he told me that I'm unique, that there is a vortex that allows me to stay connected. That must be why, somehow my being is split in three, and connected through a vortex."

"Were you connected in your first life as Jacob?"

"Presumably, as that's how I was able to create the Auditum technology. But I could only sense that Jacob's life was littered with doubts and uncertainty, trying to analyze and theorize its' way towards self-realization. But I gather that cannot be the path, otherwise why did he die? There must have been more to it, more I needed to understand before confronting Luzige, and I failed to see it in time."

"Do you know how you died in that other experience as Jacob?"

"There was a fight. Some sort of last ditch effort to stop Luzige, the Jinn that Lucious is so afraid of. Luzige and his forces were too great, and I died. Stabbed by one of his minions."

"And as James now, are you able to stop him?"

"I don't know. Lucious wouldn't answer all of my questions. I guess that's something I'll have to figure out."

# NINE

## SCORPION

"JAMES...JAMES." A VOICE whispered in his ear.

"James, wake up. He's on the move, we have to hurry," Shyla said.

"What's moving?"

"The Scorpion."

He could feel the vibrations, fast thunderous footsteps, shaking the blue rocks beneath their feet. James shot up and moved towards the cave entrance by Shyla. The Scorpion was the size of a building, at least twenty stories tall. It moved with incredible agility and speed, overturning giant boulders with ease. "Where's it going?"

"Oh no."

It began to glow a purple energy around its mouth and stinger. Sliding down the mountain, it shot at and shattered massive obstacles without hesitation.

"How are we supposed to stop this thing?" Her face was white, her eyes wide with disbelief. She leaned against the cave entrance, staring at this unfathomable monster.

"James, it's headed for the city, look where it's charging. They don't have a chance!"

"There's no way we can catch it."

"If you keep thinking like that we won't. Let's go!" She ran out of the cave, bouncing from rock to landing, sliding down the mountain in a hurry. James followed as best as he could, even though the Scorpion was miles away at this point. They were moving as fast as they could but it was impossible to catch up.

"Shyla, what are we going to do if we catch up to this thing? Did you see how it eradicated those boulders? It zapped them out of existence! How are we supposed to stop that?"

"We can't. Just do your best to get out of its way."

"That's all you can come up with?"

"I'll try to take the eyes out with arrows while you take this sword and try to stab it underneath or on top. Just be careful: that thing has claws and a tail that move lightning fast."

"I understand." James ran for a moment in silence, visualizing his moves, running through several scenarios in preparation. His actions and reactions were largely involuntary, just as they had been when he had toppled KKormak.

"James, do you see the smoke? The Scorpion has reached the city."

As they approached, they could hear the screams of the people and the yelling of soldiers at arms. They ran as fast as they could, but they were still some distance from the city.

The Scorpion had legs the size of tree trunks, supporting a grotesque, hairy, yet almost mechanical frame. It had menacing razor claws, infused with purple energy cannons, along with its deadly stinger and mouth. Its jaws were more like a circle with razor sharp teeth coming from all sides, ready to chew up anything in seconds. But most dangerous of all appeared to be its cannons, because when those lasers fired, nothing could withstand them. It was like the target literally dissolved into nothingness. James contemplated where he would go if he were hit by such a beam. Would he fade into nonexistence?

"James, I see it, it's attacking the city. People are fighting back! Come on let's go!" Shyla ran ahead, fearlessly raging into battle, not knowing what horrors awaited them. She reminded him of Tamara from his dreams. The one he fell in love with a lifetime ago. Where was she now? All of this time, stuck here in this reality, caught up in their beliefs. Something told him to question it all; being trapped in a world, a girl helping him escape. It seemed so familiar.

They ran towards the city and his eyes were not accustomed to such atrocities. It shocked him to see bodies torn in half, littered throughout the streets. But worse yet, there were so few people left. They ran in the streets, hoping to find cover or escape the blasts from this lightning-fast predator. Short screams were followed by an exacting purple energy beam. Then silence, dead silence.

Those it didn't cut in half with its claws or teeth, it disposed of with precision using shots of energy. Shyla and James hid behind a nearby building, taking cover while still being able to see its vicious attacks. It was brutal, quick, and devastating, clearing the city and intentionally exterminating the people.

"What do we do next, James?" She looked at him, her hood partially covering her face in shadows. Her chest was heaving, her words were short. She was winded, as he was.

"James, you have to focus. You can do this; I've seen you fight."

"Well that maybe, but what if that's the extent of my abilities? I don't stand a chance against that thing!"

"You have to trust yourself, and trust that you can do it. I've seen you. You have access to power. Once you access it, there are no limits."

"But what if it should fail?"

"You are prepared to fight, that's obvious. Trust in what you've been gifted with; it's our only chance. I tell you this: we are leaving this dimension today, one way or another. I have lived too long in the prison that is this reality, and I cannot stay here any longer. Either you free us, or we die."

"Understood." James closed his eyes and began to focus on a shield of energy surrounding his body. He imagined a shield that would protect him from the force of the cannons, like an invisible bubble. He focused hard on this image and could feel his body get hot.

"You're turning white!" Shyla shouted.

He felt energy flowing through the column of his spine, filling his body with vibrations of light. The feeling tingled all the way to the centre of his forehead, causing a great throbbing pressure. It didn't feel painful, but he was aware of the pulsating energy.

"It's incredible!" Shyla shouted. "There's some kind of energy shield around you, I can see it shimmering!"

He opened his eyes, and the glowing dimmed to a light emanating from his skin.

"Is it gone?" she asked. "I don't see the shield anymore."

"It's there, in my awareness. But, I can't focus as strongly as I did a moment ago and fight at the same time. I think I can extend this to you too, but you need to wait here until I give you the signal."

"What's the signal?"

"You'll know." He stayed close to the walls and began moving down the street, hoping to keep the element of surprise. The Scorpion turned down an adjacent alley, looking for more victims.

He turned the corner and saw it half crawling across the top of a building, poking through the windows with its claws and stinger. It must have found some souls hiding out, and James could hear the screaming of women and children the loudest.

He ran towards the building just behind it, racing up the stairs. The Scorpion reached for the people, but they were slightly out of its grasp, at least for the moment. He reached the seventh floor and broke open one of the windows. He stuck out his head and screamed "Hey! Hey, you ugly beast, over here!"

It saw James, turned, and lunged directly at him. James was blown back and flew down the hall as glass shattered amongst falling pictures. The cloak he was wearing shielded him from most of the falling glass, yet a few shards still managed to graze his face. The Scorpion crashed its claw through the window, snapping at James with rapid force, crunching anything in its path like twigs. It crawled across the outside frame of the building, crushing it with each step. *Okay, I got its attention.* James thought. *Now what?*

James drew his sword, but the monster deflected his blows with ease.

He stabbed his sword into the claw, which initially seemed to injure the beast, but lost his sword in the process.

Looking through one of the windows as he came into view, the monster found him and prepared its cannon. Its right claw began to shine with deadly purple energy, and James held firmly to his awareness of and belief in the shield he'd created. He began to glow as the shield itself became visible. James held his hand above his head towards the beast as it shot its cannon directly at him.

The shot was reflected.

*It worked!* He was able to create a shield with his thoughts and deflect the monster's energy. It looked at him again, fired, and again the shot was deflected off the shield and flew into the sky. Again and again, it shot, but his shield withstood the blows.

James stood firm, deflecting each blast, but the Scorpion changed techniques and began crashing its claws and tail into the building, smashing windows and crumbling walls. He stumbled backwards into a neighbouring room as the monster hurled him through some concrete, lashing out and shooting its way towards him. Without restraint it smashed through brick and mortar. James ran away but it caught him with a strike, knocking him clear across the building. James ricocheted off the walls from the force of its monstrous blow. He got up, disoriented, just as it managed to break its way completely into the building. Smashing down the hallway, it approached. James stood up and raised his hand towards it, willing it to stop.

It struck him hard enough for pain to radiate thorough his entire body. James broke through a wall and tumbled down a set of stairs. He opened his eyes, trying to recover. The Scorpion struggled to reach him but its size prevented it. James continued to roll down the staircase, finally hitting a landing, blood running down from several cuts.

*I have to get out of this building.* James gathered what will he had left and ran down the steps. He could hear the Scorpion struggling to find its way down. It was a killing machine, but it wasn't that smart. James escaped the building and saw Shyla running down the street towards him.

"I saw the laser shots flying into the air and came running! You're still alive!"

"Barely. That thing packs a punch. You need to stay off to the side and nail it with your arrows. I'll do what I can to distract it; it seems to like smashing me around so that shouldn't be a problem."

James limped down the street as Shyla ran off to take cover by some nearby buildings. His body ached and the pain throbbed through each of his limb. When he focused on it, the pain intensified, and he realized that the more he focused on it, the more he experienced it. He quickly shifted his thinking to becoming strong, healthy, and healed. His walk became more confident with each stride as the pain lessened, and his thoughts became his experience. James grew stronger with each step down the street, but he knew the Scorpion would appear any moment.

He was nearing an intersection when it burst out of the building with incredible force, causing debris to fly onto the street. It crashed down, landing only steps away from him. It stood over him and James stared directly into its eyes. Its mouth was opening and closing, waiting for its next victim. It moved with mechanical sounds and organic undertones as it moved its body to accommodate its gaze.

Somehow it understood something while looking down at James, as did he. It raised its claw above its head, preparing for its final strike. He didn't flinch as he deliberately maintained his gaze with the beast. It released a strike with lightning speed, claws open and ready to cut him in two right where he stood.

James raised his hand toward the beast as it flew at him, shining with a brilliant white light. The scorpion immediately stopped in its tracks as it stared at James's glowing palm. Quite shocked, James felt an incredible force flowing throughout his body and exiting his hand, causing it to glow. This seemed to calm the scorpion's ravenous attack, almost hypnotizing him as it moved backward onto its hind legs.

As James moved his hand, it followed him with its gaze. It let out a gentle yet disturbing mechanical churning sound, as it apparently was mesmerized with his projection of light.

"James, James, you've done it! It responds to you!" Shyla shouted.

Just then, the scorpion turned away from James, and locked eyes with Shyla. It seemed to be mesmerized by his talent, but it was easily distracted as well.

"Shyla, look out!" She noticed it too, as it aggressively turned to face her, ready to pounce. James ran towards her as he attempted to put himself between them. The light seemed to diminish as he ran, but James lunged and focused, causing a burst of energy from his hand, which once again caught the creature's attention.

"Shyla, walk slowly towards me, and get behind me. We're getting out of here." James motioned with his hand, waving it slightly ensuring it would follow his movements. It did. Once he was sure of this, James walked towards the monster as it backed up. He stopped, then moved backwards. It walked towards him also, following his every move. James walked quicker, and it moved back in a hurry.

"It looks like it's afraid of the light. It doesn't want to attack you, it's just watching you, waiting for weakness. It's stalking you, but it's cautious, fearful."

"You're right. Let's see if it understands me." James focused all of his attention on the Scorpion. "Beast! Do you understand me? Answer me!" The scorpion looked at him, and nodded yes, letting out a screeching sound.

"I want to leave this place, this reality and return to my body. Do you understand?" Again, it nodded.

"I have had enough of you creature, I choose to leave!" Out of a genuine frustration, and yearning to leave, James screamed his words and emotions with everything that he had. The light emanating from his hand began to glow with an even more intensified shimmer than ever before, as cracking lightening started to shoot out in random directions. The creature recoiled in fear and understood him clearly. Its gaze pierced through him, blinking slowly with a painful expression. In that moment, James felt sorry it; he somehow realized that it wasn't truly the enemy, it was just scared.

"Look! It's about to shoot us, it's powering up!" She was right, the claws, mouth, and tail all began to glow an intense purple. But it wasn't aimed at either of them, rather next to where they were standing. Just then, the creature shot its lasers and created a portal of energy next to them.

"Shyla, look! It's our way home!"

"You've done it, you've saved us!"

"I don't think so…" It was a portal all right, but James wasn't meant to go through it. Someone began walking towards the portal from the other side. It was KKormak!

"KKormak, what are you doing here?" Shyla screamed in bewilderment.

"I know exactly why you're here." James said.

"How do you know that? Why is KKormak coming through the portal?"

"The reason for that is very simple." James walked towards the portal, the scorpion's claws still at rest, waiting for a signal.

"KKormak is behind all of this. Aren't you?" From out of the shadowy mist walked the lizard-like KKormak with a smirk on his face.

"You're a bright one, aren't you, James? Or should I say, Lukman?" He chuckled darkly.

"KKormak, you're behind this? You've kept me trapped here all this time?"

"No, Shyla." James interrupted. "None of this is real. Isn't that right, KKormak?" His slithery gaze locked onto James, ignoring Shyla completely. "Why don't you answer her question, KKormak?"

"You know the answer, traveler."

"What are you two talking about?" Shyla cried out. James took a breath, and looked towards her, with a saddened gaze.

"I'm sorry, Shyla, none of this is real." He didn't have the heart to tell her, but he had to. It seemed wrong to let her go on like this, forever wondering. "Including you."

"What! What do you mean including me? I'm real, I've lived many lives! I know I'm real!" She began to break down, a fragile house of cards on the verge collapsing. She looked at him with tears in her eyes, asking for both help and acceptance.

"I'm sorry. I began suspecting it on our way down the mountain; this all seemed too contrived. There was something that didn't seem right, as if we were living a dream, not able to carry out our own choices. We were carrying out the story for someone else, and I realized that even you, Shyla, must have been part of it, whether you realize it or not."

"Very good, traveler, very good. You came, you defeated my guardian, and you discovered my secrets. Unlike so many before you, you did not fall prey to the guardian's wraith, nor did you give up and take refuge in one of the cities. There is no fear in you, is there? That is what he told me."

"Who told you?"

"Now, now, I can't give you all my secrets, can I?" He sneered.

"James, stop this!" Shyla screamed. "Stop talking this way, I'm real! I'm right here, why aren't you acknowledging me? I need to go home, just like you! I need your help!" She was nearly groveling, begging for his attention.

"KKormak! Enough of your tricks! Talk to me directly, before I start to get angry." James's response was cold and sharp. He had had enough. As the words left his lips the world around him began to melt away, revealing a light blue haze all around him. There was barely enough time to look at Shyla to say goodbye. She looked at him with great sorrow at the loss of the only life she'd ever known. The world was faintly there, then not at all, with only the two of them remaining. KKormak's facade also melted away, revealing a dark blue entity of lightening, crackling like static in front of James.

As he spoke, his voice now resembled a static popping sound, echoing from all around him.

"Is this what you wanted to see, traveler? My true form?"

"Tell me, KKormak, if all of this place is an elaborate illusion for your amusement, then you yourself probably can't leave. You're trapped here, aren't you?"

"You are attempting the impossible. For you cannot stop the evil that placed us here, you cannot stop a force balanced against you. You are mighty, but so is Luzige. You are forceful, but he cannot be moved. If he takes over your world, you cannot stop him. He can never be stopped."

"There is always hope." James said with confidence.

"There is always hope? The people must understand that they themselves must change, then their world will follow. If the conditions remain the same or worsen, the onslaught will continue, and cannot be stopped beyond a certain point. Fueled by fear and hatred, your world… like so many others will succumb to greed, and corruption. Search your past, you will see that it is so."

"Who is Luzige? Why does he do this?"

"He is the counter balance, the inevitable destroyer of worlds that is called forth from the depths. A portal was opened by one who is noble, and passes through to destroy a corrupt planet."

"Once called, is there no reversal to this process?"

"If you are meant to stop the process, it will stop. Only through the might of a noble soul, and those who follow can the world change its fate."

"Change it to what?"

"You are to choose complete unity, less your divisions destroy you."

"That's impossible, how are we going to overlook the problems that have plagued the world for centuries?"

"See that there is more to lose if you do not. See the commonalities, and overlook the differences… unless you cannot do so in time. If that is not your fate."

"What are you talking about? So are you saying that this is all a part of some plan? Who is responsible for all of this?"

"You are all responsible for your fate, through the choices you've made, or failed to make."

"Enough of this, you never answered my first question. You are trapped here, aren't you?"

"No, I am not, and neither are you. You were sent here as a test, and now we know."

"Know what?"

"If you stand a chance of course, many are watching you."

"Now what?" James didn't look surprised. "There is still time, traveler. Your brother Joshua is being held captive in the city, in a large tower controlled by Luzige. Rescue him, he will have the device you created on Earth, Auditum. Use this to find your friends in the other world. They will know what you must do. There is always hope."

"So I'm free to go?"

"You are always free. But first you must realize it."

# TEN

## A Forgotten Necklace

THE NEXT THING James recalled was waking up in his bed. He was disoriented, but he was definitely in George's and Jess's home. He began to straighten out. His body felt very stiff. Suddenly Jess ran into the room.

"You're awake! Thank God, you're awake! We were so worried about you!"

"What do you mean? Of course I'm awake. How long was I asleep?"

"You were asleep for seven days! We thought you had fallen into a coma. Are you okay?"

"I think so, let me stretch out a bit." He got up slowly, straightening out where he could. "Ouch, that doesn't feel too good."

"James, you're awake!" George came walking towards him, and helped him to stand. "This is very good news. We weren't sure you would come back to us. Welcome back," he said with a solid stance, his brow furrowed.

"Thanks."

A short while later they ate breakfast and James told them about the long dreams he had, and what he was supposed to do.

"James, we've talked about this. I will not stand in your way if you think this is what you must do, but please be certain of it. The way is dangerous enough, not to mention the disaster that awaits you at your destination."

"There's something inside me that beckons me to follow my dream. If I have a brother and he needs my help, then I need to find him."

"I understand. You should make your way down to the train station. From there you should be able to get anywhere in the city. But be careful, I believe that's where they put the concentration camps."

"Camps?"

"After the cities were destroyed, they blamed the Arabic people. Just like in World War II, they rounded up the Arabic people and brought them to camps, as was done with the Japanese."

"Is that what the governments did? Rounded up the Arabic people?"

"That was one of the things that happened, yes. Many people were taken as a result of the End Games incident. It destroyed our world as we knew it; borders began to melt away, and systems of harsh controls were implemented everywhere. People were rounded up and brought to camps via secret railway systems. Presumably those systems had been there for years, just waiting for an event of such significance to occur."

"What happened to all the people?"

"They were brought to processing centres and then sent to camps to live and work, or else they were jailed or killed. People were relocated in large numbers to be sorted and classified. Up here in the north, we weren't worth the trouble. We barely have internet up here, and since we have a harsh winter for most of the year, there's been no real motivation for them to come up here, lucky for us."

"So since then, what's happened?"

"We heard from people coming up from the Southlands that things began to settle down. People were slowly released, and a rudimentary economy began to develop. Life went on, but now the world is very different. That's why you need to be careful. Don't disturb the police, don't cause a fuss, and do not start fighting in the streets! Before you know it, soldiers will be all over you."

"I see what you mean. I'll try to be discreet."

"That's all I can tell you. Take my truck. It's old like me, but it'll get you far."

"No, George, I can't take that."

"It's yours. Good luck to you, my friend."

"Thank you."

"We're going to miss you!" Jess shouted.

"I'll miss you both, thank you for everything."

Jess smiled at him. He'd miss them too, but they were safer up here. He had to deal with whatever else was awaiting him down south, and hopefully he had what it took to stop it. His brother Joshua must know where the Auditum headset was. It was probably why they captured him. James needed to somehow use it in order to tune in to the other dimensions and find his friends. It was strange for him, though, to call Joshua his brother, for he had never known him while living as Jacob Cross.

He packed up his things and threw the suitcase onto the bed of the truck. His goodbyes with George and Jess were short and sweet. He'd already said what he needed to say, and so had they. There wasn't much for him to take. Some cases of water, some canned beans, and a few other supplies. The trip down was about forty hours of uneventful driving. He managed to stop a few times for gas, and slept in the truck at night. There wasn't much around, and there were fewer and fewer people as he approached the down town core, as if everyone had cleared out a long time ago. They had most likely gone inland, away from the Catalyst infection. As he approached the main artery of the city, he could see plumes of smoke in the distance. Several fires could be seen as the city burned in various pockets. In the shattered glass of old windows were signs and logos, reminiscent of companies that were long forgotten. The buildings that were once monuments to the capital of commerce were now the hive of mutated human stock. James didn't think there was anything human left there, but he was told there were shelters and camps near Union station so he continued south into the heart of the city.

There they were, the general Arab population. They stood behind a makeshift log wall, with a thick entrance, guarded by several men. James kept his car in plain sight of them, parked, and walked towards them slowly. Outside the entrance he could see tents with old woman and children scattered about. They were dressed in traditional Muslim garb, as were many people around him. This looked less like a safety zone and more like a prison, yet the gate remained open. James approached one of the men who was dressed in a black molded uniform, equipped with a menacing sword. "Halt. Where are you from? What are you doing here?"

"I'm from the North, I'm told there are many people still here, and I'm looking for someone. Can I enter?"

"Yes. Don't cause any trouble, or we'll throw you to the mutants. And you'd better do something about your car before sundown, or those things will tear it apart. There's a gate around back where you can bring your vehicle."

"Okay, thank you, I'll stay out of trouble." He gave James a look and slowly stepped aside. James walked down the dusty road, covered in dirt and sand. He looked up and saw an old street sign; it said "Bay Street." He guessed that meant something once.

There were people scurrying about, many talking, and chattering in what he assumed was Arabic. Blasting from a loud speaker was "Allah Akbar." Flags were displayed, and shops were setup. There was a little village here, regrouping after their abrupt relocation. These areas had grown into cities, but it wasn't long until Luzige's reign stretched across the entire country and broke down most government controls. What was left was either controlled by rogue militia groups or Luzige.

Only a few shops with glass windows remained intact. They seemed to stand out, so James walked towards them. There was one that had the markings of an old coffee shop called "Le Bon Verve." It seemed vaguely familiar, so he walked inside. The shop's aroma reminded him of good friends and deep conversations. He paused, only for a moment as memories of a girl named…

"Sarah's the name, this is my shop, and how can I help you?" A chirpy voice from behind him caught him in his daze. James spun around, surprised by her soft features and good looks.

"Oh, hi. I'm James. This is your shop?"

"Yup, it is."

"Hey, Sarah, who's your new friend?" A grisly voice came out from the back room, as a rather large man walked out. He stood over six feet tall, with a barrel chest and a curly red beard.

"This is Sam, he works here with me." James bet he protected her as well. He looked like he'd been in a few fights not long ago. There was a strong look about him, but he was also jolly.

"I mean either of you no harm, I'm just here looking for someone. I was told I might be able to find them here."

"The only people you'll find here are mutants and Arabs. If you're looking for that, we've got plenty."

"The person I'm looking for is neither. I've been told there's a tower, and that he might be there."

"You've been told a lot of things it seems," Sarah said. "Who are you? What are you really doing here?" She was quick.

"My name is James; I've come here from the far north. I'm looking for my brother. I need to find him."

"What's his name?"

"Joshua."

She looked taken aback, perhaps surprised that James knew of him. "I know that name. If you're connected to Joshua in any way, you shouldn't be here. He's a terrorist."

"What do you mean a terrorist?"

"He's an enemy of the state."

"The United States?"

"No, that hasn't existed in years. I'm talking about Luzige. If you're against Luzige, you're a doomed man. And that's Joshua. He's a hero, mind you, because he continues to try and disrupt their supply routes, and training facilities, but he's only a small force."

"But you called him a terrorist."

"That's what you're called when you're not conforming. You are labelled an outcast and called a terrorist. You are dehumanized, separated from the rest. That's how soldiers are convinced to murder other humans, and this is how populations are controlled. If you associate with a known terrorist, you will be targeted as well."

"I see. Do you know where they are keeping him?"

"If he's in this city, the main control tower is up the street. The largest office tower left in the city is being used as a base for Luzige. If Josh is in this city, they'll have him somewhere in there. But that place is heavily guarded. I don't know how you'll get in there."

"I'm not sure either."

"So you've come here without a plan and without any weapons, I presume?"

"Pretty much."

"Well we can't help you here, but there's someone who can. He's an arms dealer, but you can't bring him in here. This shop is all I've got left, and I'd like to keep it intact."

"I understand. I won't bother you again."

"No, that's not what I meant, I…he's across the courtyard, south of the broken statue. You'll see a dark corridor and at the end of that you'll see a red door. Give them this." She quickly wrote a note, and placed it within a yellow envelope, then secured it with a red candle wax seal. She finally handed the letter to James. The seal looked familiar, and it reminded him of a shimmering sun.

"What's this?"

"This is a letter, with the Arabe'en seal on it. That's how they'll know to trust you."

"Who are the Arabe'en?"

"The Arabe'en are an underground organization that are trying to stop Luzige. They aren't as strong as they once were, and they have mostly disbanded since their leader was executed."

"What happened?"

"Their leader was a man named Paul. In the Arabe'en language they called him Boulos. He helped us greatly, and we loved him very much. He was a visionary. He warned us, and told us all about the coming of Luzige to our world. He tried to stop it…"

"How?"

"He believed that he'd found Lukman, a traveler from times long ago, reborn to battle Luzige once more. He was supposed to stop Luzige, he was supposed to be our hero. But the man he found failed him. In a moment of desperation, Lukman attacked Luzige and was overwhelmed. Paul's champion died, and with nothing left with which to defend himself, Paul was easy prey. Luzige captured him and, when no one was looking, he was executed. He was found on an upside down cross in the middle of the Arab prison camp near old New York."

"That's horrendous, why would anyone do such a thing?"

"His execution was a message to the rest of us, a message that we should fear Luzige. And we do."

"So Paul was the last leader of the resistance? Then who am I going to see?"

"He was the last *great* leader, yes, but the resistance is far from dead. They are now lead by a good man named David. He carries on in his name, accepting the willing and able-bodied. The Arabe'en of today are also brutal and vicious, not like they used to be. Now they strike from the shadows, or else they'll end up like Paul."

"I'm going to find these Arabe'en, and I'll see if they can help. Thank you."

"Not so fast. If you make it there and back alive, I need you to bring me something."

"What's that?"

"There's an old necklace: it has a teardrop of gold with a diamond in the centre. I lost it, and I need it back. It belonged to a friend."

"Sounds familiar. They have it?"

"Yes, they have it. It belonged to someone very special, and I'd like it returned to me."

"I'll see what I can do." James walked out.

James headed toward the Arabe'en hideout, but the city itself seemed entirely different from what he was used to. Even after driving through several ghost towns, nothing seemed as strange as this. The streets were covered with sand and dust. Military fencing blocked off sections of the streets. Large walls surrounded parts of the city, keeping prisoners in, or perhaps intruders out. James still had yet to see any mutants, but he was sure they were around.

"Hey, watch it." A billowing voice echoed from above him as he bumped into a mountainous man.

"Oh I'm sorry, I was distracted and didn't see you there. I mean, not that I shouldn't see you there, you're a big guy, it's just that I wasn't looking."

"You think you're funny?" This wasn't going well. James looked behind him, and spotted the dark corridor Sarah was talking about.

"No I'm not trying to be funny, I just got here and I was looking around..."

"Abdulla doesn't like you." A crowd began forming around them and James didn't think the man was going to let him pass very easily. He must have stood nearly seven feet tall, with shoulders nearly half as wide. He was wearing a turban and a dust covered vest with a sword at his side. He took a step towards James.

"I'm sorry, Abdulla. I'll just be going now."

"You'll be dead!" He lunged with a swing of his sword, but James manoeuvred out of the way.

"Easy, big guy, I'm just here looking for someone. There's no need to fight."

Abdulla swung around, lashing out with his sword, all muscle and furry.

"You think you're smart by running away like that? Fight like a man!"

"I'm not trying to fight you, Abdulla."

Abdulla slashed at James once more, knocking him down with the butt of his sword. He stood towering over James, his expression barely visible except for his white eyes and mouth full of teeth.

James grabbed his jaw, checking to see if something was broken. "Nice one, Abdulla." He looked up at the man who was panting like a wild dog and clutching his sword in one hand.

"You still want to go through with this, huh?" No response from Abdulla.

James smiled and nodded. By this time the entire city square was watching. James could hear people in the background whispering, "Nobody stands up to the Butcher…"

James stood up, measuring off his distance between them, and settled loosely into light fighting stance. Abdulla lunged once more with a single blade strike which James easily avoided. James side-stepped and kicked the back of Abdulla's knee, collapsing him quickly to the ground. James stepped to his other side, as the man looked around, trying to figure out what was going on. James walked in closer and landed a direct strike to his temple, sending him crashing to the floor. That much force would normally kill a man, but James figured with someone his size, he would at least be knocked out for a while.

The crowd could be heard gasping as James got up and quickly ran down the tunnel towards the red door, not knowing what would face him on the other side.

# ELEVEN

## THE LAST ARABE'EN

H E GOT CLOSER to the door, noticing corroded paintings of clowns on the walls. The hallway was dimly lit, and James could hear the crowd venturing after him. James removed the envelope from his back pocket and clutched it firmly. It was the one he had received from Sarah.

James knocked on the rusted and weathered red door. The force of his rapping echoed down the hall. He took a deep breath, assumed a neutral posture, and prepared to move if need be. He heard a rustling on the other side and knocked again.

The mail slot creaked open. James inserted the envelope, still not knowing the message it contained. He heard locks being unfastened, followed by the sounds of rusted metal gears grinding into position.

The door opened revealing a dark hallway that led to what resembled a market: several rooms with people coming and going. He could hear the cries of babies in the distant background. Some people scurried across the corridors, while others walked confidently. Armed guards held positions at key intersections, ensuring some semblance of security. The living conditions were not fit for humans, but they survived, suffering more than living.

A large man stood by the door, grasping the envelope James had given him. He held an assault rifle over his left shoulder. He wore a purple turban and had a large thick beard.

He spoke. "You are seeking David, yes?"

"Yes, I am."

"Come with me." He walked passed him, making his way through the hordes of people. There were many women, half dressed and dirty. They began looking at James and some reached for him, speaking in a language he couldn't understand. They pulled at him, bringing him towards their rooms. James recoiled.

"What's wrong, you don't like girls?" The guard laughed, as they walked by. James looked at him sharply and continued on.

"Who are all these girls? What are they doing here?"

"They work here." He said. As they walked, James could see some people smoking water pipes through the windows of their cement huts. It must have been some form of narcotic, as they puffed and fell backwards onto their pillows.

"What are they smoking?"

"They are smoking C of course."

"And what is that?" He didn't answer James's question. Instead he led him to another hallway with a dimly lit room at the end of it.

"Wait here." He removed the envelope from his pocket, and proceeded through the sheet hung in the doorway. James could overhear them speak. The guard came out again.

"Go, David is in here." He turned around and walked away. James went in, and found a modest lodging. Books were neatly organized on a table, with a yin-yang symbol carved into the wood. James recognized it from an old I-Ching George had back at the house. There were swords decorating the walls, different than the scimitars he saw used by the Arabe'en.

A flicker of candle light caught his eye, as he saw an older man sitting at a table, writing away. His eyes looked gentle, and his face looked happy. He reminded James of someone he once knew, but he couldn't recall who.

"Are you David?"

"I am. And you're James?"

"Yes. I was told you could help me."

"Ah, our mutual friend Sarah told you that, right? I know what she wants."

"Are you able to help me?"

"I don't know yet, but I know one thing."

"What's that?"

"I can't give you that necklace, James, and she knows that."

"Why not?"

"That's not just any necklace. It was worn by Lukman himself; it's all we have left of him. It's not even her necklace. It's an artifact of the Arabe'en now."

"I see. Why does she want it?"

"She loved him, and she wants something to remember him by. But I can't give it to her, it's too important."

"The note, what did it say?"

"Here, read it yourself." He passed Sarah's letter.

"Don't kill him, James must speak with David." David read aloud from memory. "Signed Sarah."

"How did you know it was the same Sarah?"

"My dear friend, there is only one Sarah." He got up and approached James. He was larger than James, standing nearly six feet, two inches tall. He did not tower over James, but he had girth.

"What can you tell me about Lukman?"

"Well." He laughed. "He is a modern saint, maybe the last one. A man who transformed and became something else, something that almost stopped that demon. Lukman is the name given to him by the Arabe'en, my people. We were once governed by an enclave of elders, when times were brighter. The Arabe'en were once a spiritual group, intent on finding the way to peace and balance. That was before I joined them, that was when they were led by a spiritual warrior named Paul."

"So how did you get involved?"

"In the earliest days of what was called the End Games, all cities collapsed, but we still don't know why. Many buildings imploded right where they stood. Much like a controlled demolition, each building fell, killing millions around the world. The Arabe'en were implicated as terrorists, and rounded up into camps for detention and processing. It wasn't long after that anyone with Arabic decent also became a threat to the state, and that's when I was captured. I'm Egyptian."

"What did they do to you?"

"You cannot understand what it's like to live under such conditions. If you are to survive at all, you must wall off your emotions. You may have some compassion, but only to extend to someone you can actually help. Otherwise, you must see everyone as a ghost, an illusion, or else you'll go insane. You cannot endure so much suffering all around you for so long unless you convince yourself that it's not real." There was a great deal of sadness in his eyes, but his face was serious and cold.

"I'm sorry." James said with sincerity.

"Aren't we all? Either way, it was only once I arrived in this God-forsaken place that I actually made contact with the Arabe'ens. They lack people who can translate and speak both Arabic and English fluently, and a voice to keep them together. It wasn't long before I grew in my ranks here. They were lost, and needed someone to lead them, so I stepped up. We're all very different now."

"And what are you now?" James asked.

He smirked. "We are warriors, fighting to help those around us, and keep our traditions alive."

"But your home doesn't exactly have purely Arabic decoration. Your table has the Taoist symbol of Ying Yang."

"Very perceptive, James. I was not always leader of these people. I had a much different life before Luzige entered our reality. I lived a life of imbalance, to say the least. I drank and I enjoyed women, but I did not do much of anything else."

"What changed?"

"I had a close friend for all of my life. He was very dear to me and kept me from killing myself on some occasions, whether he realized it or not. When I lost him, everything changed, and so did the world around us. When Luzige arrived, he brought hell along with him. Lukman was the only one who stood up to Luzige seven years ago. And because there was no one else in his way, that monster destroyed everything, our whole civilization."

"But Lukman stood up to him?"

"Yes, he fought him. We never knew something like that was possible, the way he could fight. But then again, we never thought we'd see mutants running around killing people either." He laughed.

"So what happened?"

"This is how I remember it, although people have already started forgetting how it really was. No one writes anything down anymore, so I try to when I have time. Essentially, everything was normal, and within a short period, maybe forty-eight hours or more…maybe three days, everything went to hell. Big cities became overrun with huge deformed mutants, like lizard people…some were like dogs, and the worst were some combination of human and beast. The streets ran with blood, as these merciless creatures feasted on all the flesh they could find. They shied away from the light, but—even still today—they own the night. That's why the cities have gates around them…to keep mutants out."

"Why did these monsters start walking the earth? What happened?"

"That's where everyone's stories start to differ. Some say it was the Auditum technology, a frequency or sound wave system that came out of the Netex Corporation. Or the government was behind it all… that's a popular one. Some say they even tried to use Auditum to stop the creatures. Others say it was the Catalyst drug that was put into the water supply and messed with human growth hormones. And the more religious among us say it's the work of the devil. Hard to argue with that. Either way, Luzige was responsible on some level, that's for sure."

"So why was it only Lukman that went up against him? No police or military? What happened to the world's armed response?"

He burst out laughing. "I like you, James, you're hilarious. Why don't you know any of this? Are you from outer space?" The laughing continued.

"Actually I don't remember anything, something happened to me."

"So you have amnesia or something?"

"Something like that yes."

"Well, to answer your question there was no time to mobilize a response. At the time, we didn't even know who we were up against. At first, we thought Luzige was a terrorist organization. It was only until after he had us by the balls that we discovered it was actually a man, if you can call him that."

"And Lukman?"

"The world was brought to its knees in six days. But on the seventh day, there emerged a glimmer of hope. Sorry, James. This is where it starts to get a bit poetic." He chuckled. "This is the story we tell our children to help them sleep at night while the monsters pound away at our walls."

"It must have been very tough. It still looks tough."

"And what about you, James? You don't know any of this? Everyone knows these stories. Where have you been? On a desert island?"

"I've been in the North, and I don't remember my past, only pieces. But right now I know that I need to find my brother, Joshua. Can you help me?"

He stroked his chin, grinned, and smiled. "Why not? There are lots of people with lots of stories. So you forgot your past? Good for you! I should be so lucky! I will help you how ever I can James, because I like you. But memories are like dreams. At certain times, they feel very real, but other times they feel like they never happened. Be careful you're not following a figment of your imagination."

"Thank you, but for now this is all I've got. What else happened?"

"It began with a rumbling, a gentle breeze from the north. The breeze picked up speed, followed by a vibration in the earth and then a light. The brightest light anyone's ever seen, as if the sun was walking down the street. It was a man, and he shone with brightness as he walked confidently from the horizon towards Luzige's castle. The city around him was destroyed, but he walked as if he was the last hope of humanity manifested in bodily form. There was a great battle, and, as the story goes, he toppled Luzige and had nearly won, but was betrayed in the end. He was stabbed in the back when he was vulnerable, and he eventually died."

"What happened next?"

"Luzige took over the world and has tormented us ever since. We have found some sort of middle ground in the meantime, though. We try to resist and create our old world in small pockets. We survive and always remember that it's important to laugh." He laughed again.

"Where did Lukman come from?"

"No one knows. He came out of the ashes of our city and fought like a lion. I once had a friend named Jacob, but he was killed by Luzige. Whatever happened to him in the days leading up to his death, he was different. Something had changed him, and it could have been the technology he was working on. I always suspected that maybe he was Lukman, but no one could be sure."

"David, thank you for your help. It's time to go get my brother." David walked over to a closet, opening it to reveal a wall full of weapons. He looked at James with the first serious gaze he had seen from him.

"Alright, but where we're going, we're going to need help. Let's go get Sarah." They made their way back towards the exit. He asked David about the people smoking.

"They're smoking C. That's the street name for Catalyst Compounds, the mutagenic drug that is in our food and water supply. In pure form, Catalyst Compounds can give you an extreme high, right before it kills off many of your brain cells. In large doses, it affects the pineal glands in a terrible way, causing mutations."

"So why do they smoke it?"

"People need to escape. That's why they're here. C is always easy to get a hold of. It's in most of the water. You just need to boil it off, and the residue sits right at the bottom. People have turned it into a street drug."

"That's horrible."

"Yes, but if you believe you can't control anything in your reality, it's better to escape. Or at least they think so."

"I think it's better to change your reality to something more livable."

"That's easier said than done for most people."

"Fair enough." They walked on in silence.

As they headed back towards Sarah's shop, the night sky began its dark ascent. "David, what is it about these hordes of creatures that people are scared of? What if they made their way towards the city?"

"Those creatures are looking to feast on the last few glimmers of light they can find. Namely, us, if we're still around when they get here," David said, in a matter-of-fact manner.

As they approached her shop, James could see three men speaking with Sarah inside the shop. They didn't look like the friendly sort, and Sam was nowhere to be seen. She was shouting at them, and the men were moving in. Both David and James picked up their pace.

They were brandishing weapons, a large knife and some pipes. It was clear they were poised to attack. David and James ran to her aid, still several hundred yards from the shop. Sam ran in from the back room, leaping in front of Sarah, shielding her from their blows, taking a harsh strike to the head. He went down hard.

They grabbed Sarah, ripping her clothes off. She fought back, but James and David could see that in only a short matter of time, Sam was dead and Sarah was being violated. They crashed through the door. David lunged towards the man to the right, slashing towards them with a knife. James was left to fight the remaining two men. A large brute with a pipe approached with a fast velocity, striking towards James's head. Yielding down and around him, James took out the man's ribs, followed by a flurry of precision strikes to his throat, jaw, and temple, sending him crashing to the floor.

The last assailant, still attempting to get his pants up from around his ankles, stumbled backwards, tripping over himself. Sarah fell to the floor, unconscious. There would be no mercy for this one.

He got up, tying his pants off around his waist. He pulled a knife out of his pocket, which James quickly batted away, followed up by a flurry of strikes to his face and chest, knocking him backwards. Walking in again, another set of strikes hit the man's core and head, pushing him backwards. Finally, a set of blows sent him towards David, who had a large blade ready for him. With a firm slice, it was done. His friends remained unconscious, lucky for them.

James went to Sarah immediately, covering her as best as he could. She was still unconscious, no doubt suffering a concussion from these animals. He held her in his arms, wiping away the blood from her face.

"David, get me a blanket!" They wrapped her, and lifted her up off the floor onto a nearby couch. "Who were those guys?"

"Luzige's men. They look like they'd had controlled dosages of Catalyst. They're much bigger and stronger than most of the malnourished folk around here."

"What did they want from Sarah?"

"Protection money. It's the price of doing business around here. Luzige's men are everywhere. No one is to be trusted. Many of them just cause trouble, and travel in packs. Others just run protection games against anyone still trying to run a business. Most of the time, they aren't looking for money as payment."

"I see. How did they know we were here?"

"I don't know, maybe he's been hearing about us. Spies are everywhere. But I know one thing: thanks to them, we now have access to the tower."

# TWELVE

## I Am Kane

THEY MADE A makeshift stretcher out of a blanket and tape so they could carry Sarah. "Those guys are going to have an access key-card, that's what those buildings use downtown. That's how they get back into the building," David said. James searched them both, and sure enough, he found a key-card.

"Do you have a car, James?"

"I do, I left it outside."

"You didn't park it in the underground? Those beasts out there will tear it apart."

"But it's not sundown yet. We still have time to get to the car."

"We won't stand a chance driving at night, not through that madness. Our only chance is to grab your car, and drive down through the underground entrance. This city has a huge underground shopping district which leads all the way to where they're keeping Joshua."

"Alright, let's move." David picked up Sarah—who was moaning at this point, struggling to regain consciousness—and they walked down the city streets, trying not to draw attention to themselves. The main gates were about two kilometres from where they were.

"David, she's waking up." The moaning and movement from his makeshift satchel was garnishing attention from curious onlookers.

"Let go of me, you bastards!" Her scream was muffled by the blanket.

"Shhh, it's okay, it's us," James said.

"Let me go you freaks!" She began kicking, making it difficult for David to hold his balance, nearly causing him to tumble to the floor. People were slowing down and looking at them.

"Hey, what are you guys doing?" someone shouted. The two of them moved quicker.

"David, the car's just outside the gates; let's move." Sarah wouldn't have it and continued to resist. Nearly conscious, but not listening to them one bit.

"Sarah, stop it. It's us, relax." James said. Again, she wouldn't stop.

"Guards! Grab those two, they've taken someone!" Someone called.

"That's it, we've got to go!" David and James started running down the street, knocking down people and market stands in their path. Behind them were two guards with swords in hand, who had appeared from within a nearby store. They started to chase the group of three as they ducked to the right, down an alleyway.

"James, let's go, this way! You have to take Sarah, I can't lift her anymore, my shoulder..." He strained, nearly dropping her to the ground. James touched his shoulder and was instantly sent back to a time long ago where he'd injured himself severely. He could see David playing football and being tackled from behind, sending him crashing to the ground. He used his arm to brace himself, which popped it right out of its socket, tearing the tendons and ligaments completely apart.

He watched David clutch his shoulder with his right arm. "Old sports injury?" He asked

"Yeah, how did you know?" David was puzzled.

"We'll talk about it later. Let's get Sarah out of this thing." They untied her.

"Sarah, are you okay? We have to go, those guards are right behind us." She looked at them, her face changing from terror to relief. She sprang up and hugged James, then David.

"I'm okay, thanks. What guards?"

"Can you walk?" James asked

"No, I can't."

He grabbed her wrist, and threw her over his shoulder. "Come on! We have to get out of here." They started running farther up the street, ducking through a few buildings, as they made their way towards the gate. The sun was going down, and they weren't going to make it. They took a break in a building near the market, finally losing the guards.

"James, we've got a problem."

Panting, James looked at David. "What now?"

"Look outside." He turned towards the hollowed out window a couple of stories above them. They were in a storage loft with all kinds of merchandise, manikins, and boxes. James looked outside and saw the moon taking its place in the night sky, shining light through the window.

"It's night."

"Yes."

"David, what are we going to do?" Sarah asked. "Are we safe in here?" Her face was bludgeoned and tired. She would be recovering from those brutes for a while yet. James wasn't sure how much more she could take.

"The gates keep out most of those creatures, but some of them might scale the walls. Some of them might already be in here. Either way, the only way we'll survive the night is to get to your car, James. Then we've got to get the hell out of here."

"We've still got weapons, so how bad can it be?" James asked.

"Good luck shooting something that's already dead. Bullets aren't stopping these things. Let's just hope we can get to your car before they do. Give me your keys."

"Why?"

"I'm the one who knows how to get to the tower. Don't you trust me?"

"Of course I do." James said giving him the benefit of the doubt.

"Well, then?"

James looked at David and handed him the keys. A sense of foreboding overtook him, and he felt like they were being watched.

David slowly motioned with his head, leading them towards the exit. Behind him, something made a clinking sound on the ground. A penny rolled out of the shadows towards James's feet, hitting him, and jostling on the floor. He looked intently into the darkness, but saw nothing.

"James, let's go, don't look there. We've got to move, now!" David and Sarah ran towards the exit, pulling James along. He walked backwards slowly, not wanting to take his eyes off the darkness. He didn't trust it enough to turn his back on it.

"Jaaaammmmmess….." A deep voice whispered from the darkness. A sound of footsteps was coming closer, but there wasn't anything to be seen in the darkness. James hurried to catch up to David and Sarah.

"Where are you going, Jaammmesss?" The voice grew louder again, giving a cold, quiet laugh.

"James, run, don't look into the darkness, we got to go now!" He looked toward David, and looked back at the darkness once more, just in time to see the punch coming at him, knocking him to the floor. James forced his eyes open. Above him stood a muscular, grotesque figure with grinning teeth. His skin looked burned and ready to fall off, revealing bloody muscle beneath the surface. He moved, huffing like a large ape, ready to throttle anything in its path. The next blow came from a swift kick to the side of James's head. *Boom!* The strike vibrated through his skull, yet somehow actually knocked him back into awareness.

As he slid across the floor, all he could see was this beast charging at him. He got up as quickly as possible, just in time to launch a fierce kick to its kneecap, followed by a cascade of strikes to its face and core. By this time David and Sarah were nowhere in sight. Left alone to face the demon, James knew he had to finish the job.

Its hulking arms and chest barely felt the strikes he was throwing at it. Before he knew it, he was grabbed by the creature and tossed into the air. His body slammed through a table of old computer junk and sending equipment flying everywhere. Reeling from the pain, James started to make his way through the debris, trying to gain some distance.

"You don't remember me do you, Jaaameesss? Of course you don't, you don't even remember who *you* are."

*How does it know my name?* This creature came from the shadows and looked like a demon but fought like a man. What was worse was that it knew things about him.

"You don't even remember her do you, Jaammes? The girl you let fall through the cracks he created in your dream world, your precious Tamara. It was too easy to capture her; you didn't even try to stop him. Don't you think about her anymore? How I pity her, for her hero doesn't even remember what he did to her. Have you gone cold in your heart, fearful of what you might find? She thinks about you. She cries for you. We hear her screams through the smoke and shadows. He toys with her in his chamber now." He was trying to get a rise out of him, and he was doing a good job. *Tamara, where are you?* The monster began walking closer and closer as he scurried towards the nearest exist, still recovering his wits. Trying not to make a sound, James moved towards the door where David and Sarah had gone.

"All she sees now is darkness, thanks to you. Darkness and smoke is her existence." The creature began growling and snorting like a wolf, gritting its teeth, trying to get the scent of his prey. It too emitted some sort of smoke or haze. It was also strong, really strong; James had never been hit like that before.

"You are clever, changing your body like that. But your scent is the same, I know who you are. You've hidden from us for a long time, but now I've found you. Soon his armies will pour from the mountains taking over this world and everything in it, and not even you can stop us now." James saw the door, but it was too late. The demon was already upon him. He grabbed him from the back of his neck, throwing him across the room through several tables of merchandise. The pain of his back nearly breaking against the table jarred James awake, as he was nearly losing consciousness. If he was going to survive, he'd better wake the hell up.

James saw it running towards him as he stumbled to his feet. The demon's fists smashed across his face with tremendous speed. He fell backwards, taking another punch, and then a kick to his midsection. He looked up at its face once more, and somehow from this angle, it did look familiar. Although winded, James managed to squeeze out a few words. "Who are you?"

Smiling and laughing arrogantly, the monster growled. "I am Kane." A flash of light and memories came to James, as he recalled Mark Taylor and Stephen Kane. They were Project Managers under Edward Aidan, who had eventually become corrupted by Luzige. This must be the same Kane, sent here to find him.

"What are you doing here, Kane?"

"I do what the darkness tells me. I was sent here to destroy you." He grabbed James's hair and began punching him, crushing his ribs and face with each blow.

Pausing his attack, Kane said "I saw her once. She was very beautiful. I understand why he wants her. Yet you, you don't even remember her now. How sad for you, and sad for her." Down on one knee, James felt the anger stir within him. Blood and saliva streamed from his mouth, and James clenched his jaw. Kane raised his hand for a final blow to the head. But at that moment, with almost no strength left in him, James stepped up and blocked his fist with superhuman speed. He looked the monster straight in the eye.

"I remember her." He followed with an uppercut right to Kane's chin, furiously continuing his attack. James directed several rapid-fire blows to its face and eyes, sending the monster backwards through a set of standing mirrors behind him. James followed up with kicks to his legs and groin, then his neck and temple. Kane staggered backwards, and James continued the attack. Finally, as the beast neared a window, he delivered one last blow to its forehead, sending Kane flying right through the glass. He was gone for now.

With that, he had to find David and Sarah. He limped towards the exit, and into the night. There was the rumbling of an engine, and a flash of headlights. The car came to a screeching halt a few feet away from James. It was David. He had grabbed the car.

"Wow, it's good to see you. You got to the car?"

"You were supposed to be right behind us. When you didn't follow, I figured we'd make it to the car and then come get you."

"Well you're here now, that's what counts." James looked at David with gratitude.

With the adrenaline wearing off, the pain started to return to his body. He got into the backseat of the truck with Sarah. David got in, and they took off, heading to the underground entrance. They drove for a while through the darkness, and James looked to see if other creatures were lurking in the night. Sarah was still sleeping, and he didn't want to disturb her. She always seemed restless when she slept. David finally asked, "So what happened back there?"

"Something came out of the shadows; it was a large human-like creature, but mutated." It was more than that, Kane was sent after him for a reason.

"Yes, I've seen many of those over the years. He sounds like one of Luzige's generals. They watch over different regions. They're very strong, and dangerous. People don't usually survive a confrontation with mutants. What did you do?"

"I fought him and incapacitated him."

"What? How did you do that?"

"I've been trained to deal with such things, David."

"Trained? Trained by who?"

James looked out the window, gazing up at the stars. "I don't know. What happens when we get to the tower?"

"I told you, I could get you to the tower, but once we're there it's up to you. We just have to go a bit farther through these tunnels. A long time ago, these were all underground shopping centres. You can still see the store fronts and food courts from time to time. Everything here has been ravaged, and left to rot. Most of it's all covered in dirt or worse. That's also why the trip is a bit bumpy. It was never meant for cars down here."

"I see. Those two thugs had key-cards; we should be able to use those to get in, right?"

"Yes, before the collapse, towers all over the city were filled with workers who would sit at computers and process information. In these towers, workers toiled for hours each day, sectioned off in cubicles. They required key-card access to get in and out of the premises at certain times. It was all monitored, and very controlled. It looks like they still use key cards to get in."

"Perfect."

"But that tower is huge, James, and there are many rooms. Joshua could be anywhere. How are we going to find him?" Sarah asked.

"Leave that part up to me." Said James.

Awhile passed before David said. "James, listen you're going to need my help. I know this city, and I have a bad feeling that without me, you guys won't make it out." James looked at David.

"Thanks David, we welcome your help. You're right, you know this city better than I do, so let's do this together."

"You got it."

The rest of the trip was silent. James thought he saw things moving in the shadows, or things flying overhead, but he wasn't sure. Before long, he fell asleep. Images of Tamara surrounded in smoke and ash flashed through his mind. She sat at a table lit by candle light. She wrote in a book with feather tipped pen, her hair down covering her face. The darkness and brimstone spewed ash up all around her. He could feel her fear.

"James, Sarah, we're here." James opened his eyes and saw the end of the tunnel. There was nowhere else they could go.

"It's on foot from here. This is the old Union Station subway. We can walk through the gates and up a few levels. I don't know what's in store for us, so we have to be careful. Get your weapons ready." There were turnstiles blocking the way, and it was dark, but some emergency lighting still worked, flickering in the distance.

They walked up the broken escalators and into the concourse. The cathedral ceiling was huge, revealing some amazing Early-modern architecture, reminiscent of spider webs.

"If Joshua is in this building, he'll probably be in one of the south towers. They're the biggest towers, and it's as good a place as any to start. We need to get to the elevators." They agreed and continued on, but as they exited the concourse, they noticed a large group of grotesquely misshaped humans. They looked more like large masses of flesh rather than people. There were many of them, talking to each other in a deep throaty dialect.

"Cannibals. If they see us, we're royally screwed. We have to go around." David took them behind some pillars, moving slowly as not to be seen. They arrived at the bank of elevators.

"He's in one of these towers, but each elevator only goes so far up the building."

"So which floor do we choose?"

"Knowing how egotistical Luzige is, we should probably start at the top." Sarah said, sneering.

"Good point." James agreed.

"Well, that's as good a place to start as any." The elevator doors opened and the three got on. Sarah pressed the button for the top floor, but the doors wouldn't close.

"What's going on?" Sarah asked.

"I don't know. Push the top floor button," David said sharply.

"I did. It's lighting up but nothing's happening!"

"Guys, we'd better figure this out soon because those cannibals are starting to notice us." James said.

"Try the key-cards!" David grabbed one of the cards and inserted it into the elevator access slot. The security light on the elevator panel turned green, and the doors closed just as the cannibals drew closer.

"That was close." James said.

"Yes, but now the problem is that we've alerted them to our presence," David warned. "I'm not sure what's going to be waiting for us at the top."

"We'll deal with that when we get there," said James. "Sarah, stay in the corner away from the door."

"Brace yourselves." David said firmly.

# THIRTEEN

## INFIRMARY

T HE ELEVATOR RIDE was long and silent up to the 52$^{nd}$ floor. Although he fought together with Sarah and David, James felt alone in those moments. He didn't know what faced them on the other side of those doors, and neither did David or Sarah. At least they had that in common.

"Get ready." David said as they neared the 52$^{nd}$ floor. He clutched his handgun and Sarah and James drew their weapons as well. *Ding.*

The doors opened, revealing a long dark hallway with many offices. Scattered papers were everywhere. The lights were mostly burnt out, and the rest were either blinking or gone. It was dark, very dark.

"There's no one here." Sarah exclaimed.

"Maybe. Let's move." David walked out slowly, unsure of what they might find. They looked in each office as they moved on down the hallway.

"This must have been an executive floor." James saw couches, and many luxurious things which were not completely destroyed. There wasn't a person in sight.

"Where is everyone?" Sarah asked.

"There might still be someone up here, so be on your guard. Let's look for a map, there's usually one near the fire exit." David whispered.

"If this is Luzige's tower, where is he?"

"He could be in many places." James's awareness was slowly coming back.

Sure enough, near the elevator, they found a map of the floor. "Here, is this it?" Sarah asked.

"Yeah, exactly. Hmm…" David paused. "If he's on this floor, he's probably being kept here or here." He pointed to two large rooms at opposite ends of the floor.

"Why's that?"

"Because it looks like these rooms are connected to the water mains. There are probably bathrooms or showers nearby. If you are keeping a prisoner, you might want access to water." James looked at David; he seemed a little too familiar with this place, or maybe he just knew a lot about torturing people.

"I hope you're not leading us into a trap, David." James looked him square in the eyes.

"If I was trying to kill you, I would have done so already. Are we going to get your brother or not?"

"Of course."

"If they're at either ends of the floor, should we split up?" Sarah asked.

"No that's not a good idea, not after what I faced back there in the market."

"Okay. Which side, east or west?"

"Sarah, you pick." David said.

"West."

"Alright, west it is. Let's move."

They shuffled through the corridors, tension building with each step. As they continued west, they arrived at a room that looked like an open cafeteria. It was rather large with table seating everywhere. Things were knocked over, and the lights were barely on. James looked at David and Sarah and went inside. He walked in slowly, gun in hand. The room was massive, with a capacity of at least 300 people or more, but empty. The kitchens in the distance had flickering lights illuminating a few fridges. He walked towards them.

James headed for the fridge, hoping to find a bottle of water or some nourishment. As he opened the fridge door, a putrid odour poured out, the likes of which he'd never experienced before. Inside the fridge were fetuses and assorted body parts in jars being preserved for some reason. James slammed the fridge door and Sarah drew her head away in disgust.

"My gosh, who could do such a thing to those poor creatures?" Sarah asked.

"I don't know, but let's get out of here. There's only one room left to check on this floor." They left the cafeteria, turning back down the hallway, and started making their way towards the east side of the building. The walk was quiet, but James knew better. If someone was storing those specimens, then they were there for a purpose.

They approached a large hallway. At the end of it were doors with the word "Infirmary" written across in blood. There were also blood smears on the walls, stained from long ago.

"James, what do you think happened here?" Sarah asked.

"Nothing good."

"I hope Joshua isn't in there." David added.

"Come on, we've got to find him." James walked towards the door, slowly pushing it open. There was only darkness, and a dimly lit room further inside. Moving towards it, they fastened their gear and prepared for what they might encounter. What came next would never leave his memory. Through a fastened weave of surgical sutures was an array of brutality the likes of which James could not imagine. Bodies were opened, and in other places skin seemed stitched together. Whatever happened here, these people were torn apart. Organs were freely displayed from specimens of all ages judging from the sizes. His mind felt the overwhelming terror and fear these poor people must have felt. Behind him, Sarah and David were clutching their noses and mouths, while James stood in utter disgust that such horror could be brought upon another sentient being. *Is there no compassion for those who feel as you do? Is your hatred so great that this form of torture is allowed to exist?*

He shuffled through the room slowly, dropping his gun to the floor. He saw jars of human and mutant samples being preserved. A hybrid child, tortured and ripped open yet still alive, was laid out on an operating table in the middle of the room. They must have been experimenting with Catalyst mutations. It was being kept alive by some machine pumping blood into its heart, and oxygen into its lungs. It was clearly suffering, and James disconnected the power source, allowing the creature to die in peace.

"It's okay, James, that was the right thing to do." David placed his hand on his shoulder. James turned back to look at him, and saw someone behind them. He looked like a doctor, but he wore dark sun glasses and was holding a shotgun.

"Look out!" James said as he pushed David and Sarah out of the way.

The Doctor jumped around and started to laugh, firing shots at them. They quickly took cover behind the operating table. David leaned out and fired back a few shots from his pistol. Sarah covered her ears and took cover between the two men. James couldn't find his gun.

Another blast went off, but it couldn't penetrate the metal table. They returned fire as the doctor laughed at them with an insane high-pitched squeal. He started to reload and James ran out, launching a kick to his head, which he quickly blocked. He repeated with the other leg, but was blocked again. James threw several punches at the doctor's face and body but he yielded, and deflected with his shotgun. He returned with a strike to James's head with the butt of his gun. He was unbelievably fast, and struck James with several swift kicks to the chest, back and side before finally unleashing a flying roundhouse that sent James soaring into a cabinet of surgical equipment. He was stunned as he struggled to his feet. David jumped out without fear or hesitation and fired at the doctor but was quickly disarmed. He grabbed David by the throat and threw him across the room, causing him to crash into a nearby stretcher. Sarah moved across the room and ran through the door that connected to some back offices. At least she was out of harm's way for now.

James ran towards him and continued striking, and the Doctor continued to mirror his movements. Somehow the Doctor knew exactly what he wanted to do, and continued laughing as he deflected each strike and knocked him back with an elbow to his midriff. He continued with several kicks that James avoided by blocking and moving back. He stopped striking, looked at James, and then over at David who had been knocked out. A sickening grin appeared on the doctor's face as he reached into his dirty white coat and pulled out a large scalpel. James lunged for him, but the doctor easily tossed him aside.

He turned to look at David and slowly walked towards him. James ran up and struck him from behind, only to have his fist grappled, and body thrown across the room once more. The strength and agility was unlike anything he had faced yet. He walked up to David and began cutting ferociously. James ran as quickly as he could, shoving him off of David. The doctor swung at James with his scalpel and cut his forearm. He struck again, cutting James's chest twice. James stumbled backwards, tripping over some trays. With lightning speed, the doctor stabbed him again, causing him to bleed even more.

"Once I'm finished with you and your friend, I will take my time with the girl." He laughed again, squealing with demonic delight. James looked back at David, but from his angle all he could see was a pool of blood. He didn't know what had happened to him or how badly he was injured, but he knew that David needed help now. No more of this! James had to stop this maniac. The doctor ran up quickly, kicking him across the room. He ran at him again, stabbing him in the shoulder, and throwing him once more into a bank of wheelchairs. James stood up, long enough to see the doctor charging at him with an intended death blow. He yielded, paying close attention to the doctor's movements. He paced him, dodging his strikes and keeping his distance.

If he was going to mount an attack, it would have to be now. James awaited the doctor's next attack, dodging, letting him get closer. Again he lashed out at James, and again James yielded a little closer. The doctor continued to strike at him, but James continued to move out of the way, his focus sharp. He could feel his footing getting stronger and his discipline returning. Finally, the doctor came close enough for James to tear the glasses off his face, revealing his tiny black eyes. He screamed in pain as James continued to attack his throat, neck and eyes.

The doctor stumbled backwards and James moved in to strike his ribs, cracking through several. He reeled with pain as James continued hitting and breaking anything he could get his hands on. The demonic grin on his face was replaced with a bloodied slit. Combination after combination, James continued to unleash an onslaught of strikes, punishing him for what he'd done to all of these people, what he had done to David. Strike after strike, he broke his nose, collarbone, arms, foot, and launched even more strikes to the rest of his body. James then grabbed him by the throat and ripped out his Adam's apple, sending him crashing to the floor.

The adrenaline slowly left his veins, and James realized what had just happened. He turned back to see David still breathing. He ran over to him but it was too late. His face and neck were slashed beyond all recognition.

"No! David!" James shouted as he knelt by his side. David looked at him and, with his last dying breath, nodded at James. He held him close. *My friend.*

"James." He heard Sarah from across the room. In the doorway he could see a man leaning against her for support. He was a thin, exhausted man, with blond hair and blue eyes and wearing military fatigues. James stood up and walked towards him. The man looked at him intently.

"This lady here says that you're my brother. That can't be. My brother is dead. Who are you?"

"James."

"My brother isn't named James."

"I've been sent here, Joshua; we need to get you out of here. I need your help to stop him."

"Who?"

"Luzige."

"There's no stopping him. My brother already tried."

"I know, but I'm not finished with him yet." Joshua looked at James with curiosity.

"What do you mean?"

"I mean I used to be your brother. I know it sounds crazy, but it's true. I've come to get you the hell out of here."

"Jake?" James looked at him and took a step forward, as did Joshua.

"Jake! It's you!" They hugged. "But you look different! How are you alive? Your eyes."

"Long story. And I go by James now."

"Jake?" Sarah looked at him with amazement. "You mean, you're Jacob Cross?" James gazed back at her, and she knew it was him. She hugged him, but as Joshua held onto his shoulder, James's glance crept over towards their fallen friend. He hung his head.

"Sarah, David didn't make it." She ran towards the body and cried over him. James would remember many things from that day, but none so clearly as watching her face bear the loss of her friend.

He walked behind her, as did Joshua. They wanted him back, but that was impossible now. "He was a good man, Sarah, and a good friend." James stepped aside with Joshua, leaving Sarah with a moment to herself.

"Josh, listen. They were keeping you here for a reason. You know where the last headset is, don't you?"

"James, if it gets into the wrong hands it would mean the end of us. The Auditum technology is our only hope to turn the tides."

"I need to use it. The headset will open a door to another dimension. And I need to go there, that's the only way to stop him."

"How?"

"There's a friend trapped there. His name is Tarif. He knows about the Auditum technology and the secret projects they were working on. He's the only one who had access to their files, and he should know how to stop all of this." Joshua paused and thought for a moment.

"Tarif died. How are you going to use Auditum to talk to him?

That's impossible. Are you suggesting this headset allows you to travel to 'the other side' and talk to the dead?"

"I don't know about 'the other side,' I only know there is more to who we are than just a single identity. By using the headset I can get to the worlds in-between our lives. That's where Tarif is, and I need to find him."

"Okay, I brought the headset with me, but I hid it in the ducts. I was trying to get through undetected, but they found me. I threw the headset down the air shaft, so it should be in this room near the vents." James looked around and noticed two vents at either ends of the room. "Which side?"

"Over there, on the right. Try that one." James walked over to the air shaft and picked up a nearby scalpel, using it as a screw driver. He took off the panel and crawled inside the duct.

"Do you see anything? There should be a black bag."

He looked around, and in front of him was the bag. "I see it!" James crawled forward, grabbed the bag and got out. He opened the bag, and there it was: the last Auditum headset.

"So many problems have been caused by this device." Joshua said as he looked at the headset.

"I don't think it's the fault of the technology, but rather the fault of those using it. When children play with dangerous things, they inevitably hurt themselves, don't they?"

"So what's the answer?"

"Isn't it obvious?" Sarah asked. "Take the dangerous things away from the children until they grow up. But it's too late for that now. The damage has already been done, and Luzige has unleashed his army," she said in a harsh tone.

But James disagreed with her and said, "It's not too late. There's still a chance to banish Luzige from our realm. I just have to find Tarif. I need to use this headset now." He walked over to the brown leather couch in the next room and sat down.

"Sarah, Josh, when I use this, I'll look like I'm sleeping, but you won't be able to wake me. I'm going to need you to make sure nothing happens to me because I'll be completely vulnerable."

"Is there a safer place we can go?" Sarah asked.

"I don't think so, and we don't have time. I have to do this now so we can figure out what to do next. Only Tarif knows how to stop Luzige, but there's a problem."

"What's that?"

"He's trapped, and I'm not sure how to get him out. I'll just have to see what happens when I get there."

"That's not very reassuring," Joshua said. "I think Sarah's right: I'm not liking our location. You just finished fighting off a mutated surgeon who mutilated one of your friends, and now you want to take a nap right in the middle of it?"

"Do you think we would find a safer place? Even if we get back to the car, where would we go? You know as well as I do that if we're moving during the night, those nocturnal mutants will rip our car apart. And if they don't, we might run into a band of marauders looking for food and women. It's horrible wherever we go, Josh, and we're running out of time."

"Fine, we'll stand watch." Joshua said with a stern look, reaching for a nearby gun. "But I can't be held responsible for what happens in your mind when you're unconscious." James nodded.

Sarah looked at him with a questioning gaze. "I don't know what to call you anymore, James or Jacob." She walked up to him, placing her arms around his hips and staring into his eyes. "Does it matter anymore?" She said.

"Your eyes don't look real to me. They look like starbursts. Who are you in there?" James stepped away from her, grabbed the headset and sat down.

"I'm trying to figure that out myself." He looked over at Joshua who was calmly scoping out the corners of the adjacent rooms. "You look weak. Are you up for this? I'm not sure how long I'll be out, but I'll do my best to be quick."

"You better be quick, we don't know who else might show up. I can still pull a trigger, so we're good for now."

James looked at the dials, and instinctively knew how to configure it and set the dials for ranges well into the hundreds of thousands of hertz. He placed it on his head, leaned back, and turned it on. He heard an immediate whistling and ringing that pulsed through his head. High pitched sounds loosed his consciousness from his body. Then he felt it, an energy raging through his core which rocked and shook him from side to side, yet he was stable on the couch. He began focusing on Tarif. *Tarif. Find Tarif.*

The room began to vibrate and eventually melted away. He could only see stars all around him. Then he was gone.

# FOURTEEN

## CHAMBERS

J AMES WAS TRANSPORTED into another realm, which, at
first sight, seemed like the inside of a broken-down train. There were
passengers sitting down. He looked closer at them, but their eyes were
blackened and dead. The train was rolling down the tracks at fast pace,
not stopping for anything. The electricity flickered on and off, jolting the
subway car and dimming the lights. As the lights dimmed, the people
on the train began to rise and move towards him.

The lights turned on and the train resumed, and the people sat back
down. James felt extremely cold, as if he was surrounded by death itself.
The people looked like shells of their human selves. The windows had
broken glass, and the seats were torn and covered with blood stains.
He moved down the subway car, hoping the lights would stay on. The
screeching of the wheels deafened the ears, and disturbed the train's
undead passengers. They began to notice James, slowly tilting their
heads, locking eyes with him with their soulless gazes and devilish grins.
*Where are you, Tarif?*

A wave of emotions bombarded him. They weren't his feelings,
though; they were foreign. He felt small, insecure, and full of doubt.

Thoughts would rush into his head, doubting thoughts: *Do they like me? Do they think I'm an idiot?*

*Who are they?* James thought to himself. The thoughts continued as an unending stream of consciousness. *Why don't I have the same luck as he does? Things don't work out for me.* The feelings felt forced into James, as he did not normally think this way, yet he was swimming in a sea of doubt in this reality. With their blackened eyes, the people around him looked judgemental and fearful, the same emotions he felt within himself. They were angry and full of judgement, expectation and hatred. They were frustrated with everything and everyone around them. They could see nothing except their own blinding rage and, in this reality, they lost their vision.

James made his way through the various train cars, trying not to get in anyone's way. They continued to gaze at him as he walked passed, their eyes so accusing, so hateful. To his amazement they still functioned to some degree. Eventually the train stopped at a station, and some of the people got up and left. The doors remained open, so James looked out onto the station platform. There was nothing but pillars and a lone staircase. The doors didn't close, as if they were waiting for him to leave, so he obliged. He walked through the desolate, dark station and headed towards the stairwell. He looked up, and there was a single closed door at the top. He walked upstairs towards the door and proceeded to turn the knob. It was locked.

Behind him, the train didn't move as if it was once again waiting for him. James looked back at the door and tried harder to open it. It was securely locked, so he went back down towards the train. There didn't seem to be any other way out, so he headed towards the train. As soon as he got back on, the doors closed and on the train moved once more. James had a feeling he'd find what he was looking for on this train, and somehow, the train knew that as well.

He continued walking from car to car, seeing only more disturbing examples of disconnected people. They stared at nothing at all, did they even have free will? The melancholy of this reality was overwhelming; there was a definite sense of apathy and despair as he moved. The more he looked at the people, the more they became aware of him and stared back. They were angry with him, and with their circumstances. It seemed as though they knew James did not belong here. It was becoming more apparent that they did have some limited range of free will. They couldn't see past their rage, and so their eyes remained blinded.

James had no real anger or hatred for any of these people, yet he could feel the overall impression of their dimension. He continued to walk, remembering what he was there for. He was there to find them. Tarif and Tamara were somewhere in the reality, but he didn't sense Tamara nearby. He only sensed Tarif, and he was getting closer.

James walked into the next car, but something wasn't right. He could sense that the room was shrinking, that the walls were closing in as the anger and hostility grew in those around him. James looked into the next car and saw him. Tarif, sitting there. James moved faster towards the connecting doors, yet they were too small for him to fit through. The walls had closed in so rapidly that he couldn't fit into the next car. Something was squeezing the train like a sardine can, crushing the passengers around him. They screamed, but it was too late. He had been lured into a trap. As the train pulled into the next station, Tarif moved to get off, yet James was still stuck in the train's clutches.

He closed his eyes and started to back away, retracing his steps. He could feel the world around him unbind itself and, as he opened his eyes, the train had returned to normal. He jumped off the train just before the doors closed behind him. He looked to his right and saw Tarif walking up the stairs towards the door. James raced after him.

"Tarif! Wait!" He walked through the door, closing it behind him. James ran to catch it but he couldn't. The door was locked tight, now impossible to open. *Now what?*

From behind him, he felt a tap on his shoulder. It was Lucious, coiled and ready to spring. "Miss me?" He launched a fierce punch to James's face which sent him flying down the stairs. The monk jumped after him, landing at the bottom of the staircase. "You are really difficult to get rid of, aren't you? No matter how many times I try to trip you up, dispose of you, or send you off on some fool's errand, you always come back looking for more. You're relentless and that's very annoying. You won't leave me alone, will you?"

"What are you talking about?"

"You simplistic fool; do you not see what's going on here? You're just a man on some foolish journey to nowhere. Why don't you just give up? Why don't you pack it in like everyone else and just live with it, accept it? Luzige has gained control of the world. Just bend to his will and he'll let you live. Why do you bother resisting? Aren't these matters too big for you anyway? Wouldn't you rather just sit back and let others think for you and tell you what to do? Following is easier, James; just follow his lead, like I did."

"And is your life easier now, Lucious? Now that you've handed over control to your master?" He grabbed James's throat and squeezed with demonic strength, like he could crush James's neck on a whim.

"I've been given untold strength and freedom to reign in his realms."

"Better to reign in hell than serve in heaven? Is that the phrase? How did you become so corrupted by him? What happened to you?" Lucious picked him off the ground and lifted James up by his neck, just as another train pulled into the station. The train car doors opened and dozens of people walked out, filling the platform just as Lucious hurled James towards a structural pillar.

Crashing against it, his back nearly broke in half. The people scurried around as Lucious walked towards him with great haste. James managed to get to his feet as the monk grabbed him again, tossing him against the side of the train, sending his head through the window. He grabbed him by the back and tossed him into another pillar, knocking over several people in the process. James could feel the pain of each blow, yet he was surprisingly not incapacitated yet.

"And what do you hope to achieve when you find your friends? Do you think they'll have something to tell you? Some secret? Something you didn't already know? You're wasting your time. Your friends cannot help you. They are lost, just like you."

"Shut up!" James threw a strike to Lucious's face which was easily blocked. He returned with a series of close quarter strikes that felt like several battering rams hitting him with intense speed. James could barely see, and Lucious's final uppercut sent him into a group of dark passengers.

Lucious seemed stronger, faster, and could adapt to every move.

"Do you know why you were chosen? You *were* chosen, don't forget that. You were chosen because, just like that snivelling worm Edward Aidan, you had a weak and fragile mind. So doubtful were you at the beginning, questioning yourself incessantly. So much self-doubt and fear. You were already on the verge of creating a split personality just to deal with your own fragmented realities and low self-esteem."

James stumbled to his feet, grasping the arms and shoulders of people, trying to get lost in the crowd and gain some distance. There were hundreds of people on the platform now, perhaps just what he needed to gain some separation. "What are you talking about, Lucious?"

"The Auditum technology and the Catalyst drug was just the tap you needed to go full-fledged into your psychosis. You are already a split brain personality. The LSD-like properties of Catalyst, and the Auditum sound waves only brought you to your inevitable conclusion." James could see Lucious walking through the sea of people, heading towards him at a natural pace. He was savouring his kill, no doubt.

"You know what surprises me about you, Lucious? It doesn't matter who you hurt, or how many people you betray. Nothing fazes you. You kill and destroy without remorse."

"Ah, your logical mind, attempting to influence me. Soon you will switch to your emotional self, or perhaps your physical self and attempt an attack. Do you not see how you're fragmented? Your mind was a prime candidate from the start, from your initial days with Netex your psychological screening results… all exactly lined up with what they were looking for." He hurried through a bank of people, thinking he'd found James.

"And what's that?" James emerged behind him. He turned around quickly staring him right in the eyes.

"A psycho." He launched a roundhouse punch but James deflected it, returning with a head-butt, knocking him backwards into the crowd.

The passengers surrounded Lucious, making it difficult to continue his assault. They purposely shielded him.

"Do you feel it? Are the walls closing in on you, James?"

James could hear his bellowing laughter amidst the sea of blackened eyes. He stood watchful, waiting for him to emerge at any moment. The wheels squealed as the train closed its doors and rolled out of the station. He turned for a moment to look but was greeted with a solid sucker punch to his face, causing him to stumble backwards.

"Who did that?" He looked around and only saw passengers, grinning with their black eyes, staring at James. "Where are you, Lucious?" He shouted.

"I bet that's how Tarif felt right before they killed him. Everything was closing in on him, and it was your fault."

"I didn't kill Tarif! Aidan did!" Another punch, in and out, too fast. James couldn't see it.

"You let your friend die for your sins. How can you live with yourself? And they thought *you* were Lukman? Pathetic."

James spun around, looking for any sudden movements when a kick to his midriff caught him off-guard. "Always watch your step." Lucious snarled. James looked back and again could only see passengers surrounding him in a circle. They gave him another punch to the back and ribs.

"I'm not a psycho, Lucious." He created a small amount of separation between him and the crowd that was itching to tear him apart.

"Yes, that's just what a psycho would say, isn't it?" He laughed. "Of course you are insane. Look at the evidence! You don't even know who you are! You don't know how you think. You don't know why you do the things you do or even why you are here. How did you get here, James? Do you even remember?"

"I remember how I got here. I…" The room started to spin. James could hear whispering. So much whispering.

"Do you hear them whispering about you? Do you know what they're saying? They're talking about you." The whispers got louder, but there were too many to hear what they were saying. He spun around again, trying to keep calm but the twisted demon was getting to him. James was jogged back to awareness by a punch rapidly moving towards his face. He grabbed the fist in midair before it could make contact.

"That's it. I've had enough." James tossed the person aside and began attacking anything close to him. He created a perimeter and attacked anything inside of it. James punched, smashed, and threw everyone in his way. All of the dark-eyed passengers lunged at him, but James proceeded to yield and incapacitate each one at a tremendous speed. He moved through the crowd, breaking, maiming, and ripping off body parts of any entity foolish enough to get in his way. He could feel his arms and legs get hot, white hot. His body began burning with a bright white light, and he continued to adapt and attack everyone in his path.

James quickly noticed there was no one left, and his body wound down from the battle. The white hot light dimmed, and he cooled off. James heard a noise behind him and quickly turned as Lucious emerged from behind one of the few pillars left standing in the subway station.

"Where are they?" At James's words, Lucious recoiled into a defensive posture, like a frightened lizard.

"Perhaps... Perhaps you are Lukman." Lucious scurried away. "What you've done here today has not changed what I have said. You will see," he hissed.

"Don't make me ask you again." James took a step towards Lucious, ready to tear him apart.

"At the top of the stairs, go to the door. It will open. You will find your friends, but it will do you no good."

"I'll be the judge of that."

"If you continue on, you will be greeted by death. Just as this reality was affected by your presence, you are affected by this experience. But hear this, once you've tasted death, you will be changed forever."

"Why was I brought to this place? Is this another one of your tricks?" James tensed up and was losing patience fast.

"No, this isn't my world, Jacob. It's Tarif's. I merely sensed you back in our realm and, you know me, I'm always dying to see you." He grinned.

"But why is this happening to him?"

"You're not in any ordinary realm in the astral planes. You're in Luzige's realm of despair. This is a specific sub-reality he has devised for those he chooses to torture. In this dimension your fears will come alive and, just as it is in your waking life, they will imprison you, confine you, and force you to move from one chamber to another. You think the movement you have is freedom, but you fail to see how your fears confine you."

"Where is he now?"

"He's moved onto his next fear."

"I'm warning you, stay out of my way from now on." James stared at him with savage intent until he understood, disappearing into the shadows. He turned towards the stairs, walked up and opened the door.

# PART III

## ETHER

*"You are still you, Jake. Once you became a being of light, you transcended the physical plane and entered the Summerlands. This is where we typically come from and go to after a physical life is complete. It's simply a realm where beings of a certain level of consciousness live, and a place many of us call home... It is where we incarnate from. That's where you got your new body."*

# FIFTEEN

## FROM THE SHADOWS

"WHAT ARE WE supposed to do with him now?" Sarah stood, towering over James's defenceless body, frowning.

"We have to watch him." Joshua spoke matter-of-factly like his military training demanded.

"You have to be kidding me. Someone could come in on us any minute." Sarah looked around cautiously, scowling at the buzzing and flickering lights.

"The walls are paper thin, so we should be able to hear them coming." Joshua propped James up on the couch, resting his head against a satchel. He was still wearing the headset.

"Them? Who are these guys? Are they mutants like that doctor? I've never seen anything like him in my life."

Joshua paused for a moment, and then looked at her squarely. "There's only one reason we're here, and that's this man right here. James is off in another dimension somewhere. Don't ask me how or where, because I don't know. What I do know is that he's the only one who's even come close to stopping Luzige, and he's my brother.

"Where do you think James is now?" Sarah looked at James.

"I don't know. He could be anywhere. He could have projected into his friend's reality, or somewhere entirely different. Who knows if he's even in control?"

"So should we wake him? This could be a big waste of time, and we need to get out of here!"

"Calm down and listen to me. This has to take its course. I've seen enough people using this thing, and if we interrupt the process, we could kill him."

"How do you know so much about this headset, about James, and everything else?"

Josh took a deep breath, sat back in a nearby armchair, and rubbed his brow. "I used to work for the government, that's how."

"Used to?"

"Yes, I started out as military, but once they realized I was good at math I was considered for the KIA, a covert group that specialized in psychological warfare. Also experimental technologies. Edward Aidan was a part of the KIA at some point, but that was before my time of service. The agency disbanded, and I went rogue. I looked for Jacob, grabbed what I could of Auditum tech, and tried to organize a resistance."

"That didn't go so well did it?"

"No."

"Is there any form of government left that you're aware of?"

"What's left of the government is run from hidden bunkers, deep in the mountains. I hope they're mounting a defence. But for what? Everything around us is Luzige's now. He's taken over."

"He doesn't have everything, does he? I heard there were still islands in the South free of his control."

"He has everything, Sarah. I have seen what he can do. He's unstoppable. If there's some place he hasn't taken over, it's only a matter of time before he does." Joshua said plainly.

"So why are you helping us?" Sarah asked.

"Because there's nothing else left to hope for. If weapons can't stand up to him, then maybe there's another answer. We've tried everything else. Maybe the Auditum technology has something to do with all of this, and if we're lucky maybe it can send this ass-hole back to his own dimension."

"I hope so."

"What about you? Why are you helping him?"

"Because he helped me."

"Like he helped your friend David?"

"That's different. He couldn't save him. That monster was too fast. He tried to get to him, but it was too late." "But that's what I'm afraid of. If we can't take on some mutated, sadistic doctor, then how are we going to fair against Luzige's horde?"

"Stop talking like that. Let's talk about something else."

"Fine. How did you know Jacob?"

"He was my brother. Well, my half-brother. He didn't know about me, and neither did Jake's mother until much later in life. I was nineteen when I met her in person. She was a very kind lady at first, who then politely told me to never interfere with her life or her family ever again. I listened, and joined the military instead."

"I'm sorry."

"Don't be. I learned a great deal from that experience. I learned that acceptance comes from within. No one can give it to you, and even if you get some, it is short-lived or in small, infrequent portions. I learned to be accepting of who I am, regardless of what anyone has to say. If someone has a problem with me, I have no issue dealing with that too."

"What do you mean, physically?"

"If it comes to that."

"So you've hardened up? Won't let anyone in, is that it?"

"No, that's not quite right. I let people in. I give them a chance, but I have a keen eye for bullshit."

"Fair enough. So before today, you had never met Jake?"

"We met once, but he didn't know who I was. I was in civilian attire, and I was following him. I have to admit, I was curious. For years, I never approached him, out of respect. But one morning I talked to him over a newspaper he was holding.

"Then what?"

"I walked away and went back to work."

"Big risk, wasn't it?"

"It was a risk, yes. But he's my brother."

"What about the headset?"

"During my time in the military, I was recruited for a covert defence department project by the KIA. They called it 'Project Auditum.' It was to be used as a way to create the perfect soldier, a super soldier capable of rapid healing and rampant muscle growth with a mind under complete control. They couldn't do this using the headset alone; they needed a chemical agent called Catalyst to stimulate growth hormones, like a Super Steroid. The drug had to be administered either in water or in food. For selected targets, we had to make sure they were taking their proper doses."

"So Jacob was an experiment, and you helped them ruin his life?"

"I had no choice, Sarah. None of us had a choice. This was way over our heads. People asked questions, and they disappeared. At least I was able to watch over him. I made sure they wouldn't kill him with that shit. He only had a few doses, not the full amount."

"Why the headset? What's the purpose?"

"The headset controls the thought patterns of most users to the point of reducing them to a clean slate for programming, a much more effective form of mind control."

"But this doesn't work on everyone, right?"

"Correct. Not all users were affected the same way. It affected a very small percentage of people completely differently. Jacob was one of those people."

"What happened to him?"

"As far as I can tell, it caused him to evolve."

"Evolve?"

"Do you know how long it takes for DNA to change? In a mosquito, there are two parts to the DNA. One part takes one million years to change, and the other part takes four million years to change. So it's safe to say that a mosquito has looked the same way for about four million years."

"How long have we looked the same then?"

"A long time, easily a million years, so our DNA is fundamentally the same as people walking around a long time ago."

"Okay, I'm following you so far."

"Jacob's DNA is different. Through some combination of Catalyst, and ultra-sonic sound from that headset, he's now different. Auditum caused some change at a very fundamental level. He's able to do things we can't. He's stronger, faster, and he's somehow able to tap into unlimited knowledge. He's god-like now, whether he realizes it or not."

"What kind of powers?"

"I don't know exactly. I don't even know if he's aware of his abilities just yet. But people witnessed and reported a being of light fighting with Luzige right before he unleashed his terror into the streets."

"So Jacob was that being of light? Is that what you believe?"

"Yes, I do. I think the headset causes first his brain to vibrate then his entire body, both at such a rate that he actually became light itself. That's what happened at the height of his Auditum usage, just before he died. Prior to that, he was having all kinds of experiences. Telepathy, remote viewing, out of body experiences, you name it. Auditum triggered some kind of cellular level evolution, changing who Jacob Cross was forever."

"But even with all this power, he fought Luzige and died, didn't he? How can this be Jacob?"

"That's what I thought too, until I saw him again. He was calling himself James, but he knew he used to be Jacob. He looks a bit different, but it's him."

"How can this be? Who is he now?"

"I don't know how he came back; maybe he's able to reform himself out of light. I have no idea. All I know is he's my brother, and I love him. And now that he's back, we've got a shot."

"He once mentioned a woman, Tamara. Who is she?"

"There were people who spoke about a parallel war in another realm. While we were facing demonic beings, there was another war happening as well, a much more important one."

"What do you mean?"

"Luzige comes from some other dimension. There were whispers among the Arabe'en tribes that this parallel war was with three of earth's champions battling Luzige himself. They tried to stop him, but like us, they failed. The Arabe'en believe that's what's causing all hell to break loose."

"What does this have to do with Tamara?"

"According to the Arabe'en, she's one of the three. So is James. The Arabe'en were a tribe of people, they were of Sufi decent. They were keepers of a prophecy that foretold of Luzige, The Locust, and his battle against Lukman."

"Were?"

"The scrolls are gone now, rounded up, just as many other artifacts were during the End Games. The last synchronized terror event before Luzige took over with his forces. We know now that this was all Luzige's doing, the destruction of all those cities. But it's too late now; so much has been lost already."

"Are there any left?"

"Some yes, but few reveal themselves. They still think Lukman is coming to save them. It's insanity if you ask me; the world is already destroyed. There's no saving it now. Besides, they're just keepers of an ancient belief system now. Any semblance of their culture is now gone. We've taken their land, moved them out, and rounded them up for imprisonment or worse."

"What was the government supposed to do? They were the enemies as far as they could tell."

"The same thing we always do, perpetuate violence and wars. We make so many enemies."

"But the wars were to stop the governments who hurt their own people. That's how everyone created peace, or tried to anyway. That's what my mom used to tell me when I was a little girl."

"Perhaps, but maybe we could have spent less time fighting them and more time feeding them." Suddenly, a box on a nearby desk dropped to the floor, spilling its contents everywhere.

"What was that?" Josh stood up, readying his firearm. He slowly approached the desk. As he manoeuvred behind the old wooden chair, he saw the culprit.

"It's a rat. Don't worry Sarah; it's only a ra—" He was knocked off his feet by some kind of feral corpse before he could finish. It sliced him across the face and torso, and collapsed back into the shadows.

Sarah screamed. "Josh, what the hell was it? Where did it go? James, you have to wake up!" Sarah slapped James across the face.

"It's not going to do you any good. He's long gone. We're on our own. Stay with him and shoot anything that moves." Josh leaned up against an adjacent door frame, the light flickering above him.

"Quiet," Sarah whispered. The creatures scratching across the floor could be heard from across the room.

"Did you hear that?"

"Yeah, it's coming from over there." Sarah pointed towards the next office, a few doors down the hall. Josh slowly made his way towards the noise. The scratching could be heard in a different room now.

"Wait, where did it go? I can hear it over there now. It's getting closer."

"Josh get out of there, get back into the light!" Josh took one step into the darkness and was immediately grabbed, and hurled into the shadows.

"Josh!" screamed Sarah. "James, you have to wake up!"

From the darkness, Josh emerged, running towards Sarah. "Quick, we need to move!" He gathered up their stuff, heaved James over his shoulder, and made his way towards the stairs.

"What the hell was that?"

"I don't know, but it was fast. I couldn't see it in the dark, but it cut my side pretty deep. I managed to throw it off me. We have to get to the car, now!" As they made their way down the half-lit staircase, far away footsteps could be heard above them. There were more of the mutants and the footsteps continued to multiply.

"If we can get to the car, we'll be okay and should be able to make it back to setup camp before sunrise."

"But it's night. We'll be driving through those things. We don't stand a chance if we—"

Josh interrupted. "I know, but we don't have any other option. We can't stay here, or we're as good as dead."

"Fine, we'll take our chances out there. You better drive like hell, though. We can't get stuck out there or we're just as dead."

"I know, Sarah. I know."

They made it down to the parking lot, which was guarded by a group of mutants. "The only way we're getting through here is by the shadows," said Joshua. "Sarah, hug the walls and head towards section D. Don't make a sound." She gave Josh a doubtful glance but she proceeded towards the car. They did their best to drag James's near-lifeless body with them. They momentarily caught the attention of one of the more massive brutes, but he lost them in the darkness. They found the car and got in slowly. The noise of the engine starting alerted the mutants who quickly scurried over. Joshua revved the engine, startling the mutants as they drove full-speed towards the streets and into the night.

As Joshua drove onward, he grimaced from time to time. "Josh, are you okay?" Sarah asked. "Let me see your side."

"I'm fine. We have to keep moving."

"You're no good to me dead; I can't do this by myself. Let me see, please." He looked at Sarah, knowing what would come next. She pulled Josh's shirt up, revealing the large gash he'd been hiding. "This is serious! What do I do?"

"Same thing I've been trying to do, keep pressure on it." Sarah took off her blouse, ripped it into shreds, and started tying them together.

"Sarah, I appreciate the gesture, but I have to drive."

"Very funny, keep your eyes on the road. I'm making you a make-shift bandage; we have to stop the bleeding."

"Sorry, I thought I'd lighten the mood a bit."

"It's not helping. Take your shirt off."

"Not that easy while I'm driving. Here, hold the wheel." They managed to tie a bandage around Joshua, which stopped the bleeding.

Sarah sat back in her seat and turned around to look at James. Speaking softly beneath her breath she said, "Wherever you are, James, I hope you're having a better time than we are."

Joshua wasn't looking great even though they'd done what they could to stop the bleeding. He needed to rest, and properly stitch up his wounds, or else Sarah and James would be on their own. He knew Sarah couldn't handle that, so he did his best to hang in there. He thought of what James might be going through in the other dimension. Did he feel pain there?

# SIXTEEN

## FRACTURED

JAMES FOUND HIMSELF walking through a dark forest. There were no stars or even discernible moons in this place to help mark his path. He could see only a few feet in front of him, with shades of darkness growing denser as he looked around. The trees themselves lacked leaves and, for the most part, looked rather dead. It was cold and windy. He could hear a storm coming as thunder crackled through the trees.

As he made his way through, James thought of Tarif. In the Summerlands, James saw him in his exploration of Jacob's past. He sacrificed a great deal, and was a dear friend in his former life. However, something changed near the end. Events at their workplace distanced Tarif from Jacob. He could always rely on him in a crunch, but Jacob came to realize that he chose a different path.

Lightning shot through the sky, giving him ever so slight a glimpse of his surroundings. In the distance, he saw a clearing through the bush and headed towards it. This was not like his other experiences in these realms. He felt dense, and somehow his sensory perceptions were dulled, which could have been a side effect of the Auditum headset.

James couldn't see straight after a while. There were no flight capabilities here either. He didn't like it, feeling alone and weak, but he continued onward.

The first time James met Tarif, he went by a different name, Faried. Soon after coming to Canada, he found Tarif easier for people to understand and pronounce, so he changed it. Tarif was a much different man when they first met, with many dreams and aspirations. They both were. Those dreams were dead now.

Something wasn't right. There was music that sounded like a harmonica in the distance. It could barely be heard over the thunderous roars of the approaching storm. Lightning snapped once more and, through the clearing, James saw a man in grey, ratty clothing. He looked at him briefly and slowly walked back into the forest.

"Tarif! Wait!" James shouted, but as darkness fell Tarif disappeared along with his sight. James heard music, a piano this time, and it was loud. It sounded like an old track from a Western saloon. It faded away as the lightning once more revealed a different man walking the perimeter of the forest clearing. He wore a top hat and a fine black coat, and he was holding something. The music stopped completely, but as the lightning snapped, it revealed two more people. They appeared out of nowhere and ran towards James. He raced across the forest clearing, dashing through the underbrush in an attempt to gain some separation.

They kept up the chase; Top Hat revealed a machete and a large grin with jagged teeth. James turned and saw a ghoulish female wielding a knife who was wearing the tattered remains of a wedding dress. They surrounded him and attempted to flank his position, so he took off through the forest.

A large brute smashed through trees while Top Hat kept coming, cutting through everything in his way. James couldn't see the girl and for some reason, he began to lose perspective. Walls were closing in on him. Who were these ghouls, and who was the grey man in the distance? He could hear the disturbing sounds of a fiddler beyond the clearing so he ran away from it. The three were hot on his trail, running and vaulting over trees, but James was still able to keep ahead of them.

The large brute was massive. He looked like an oversized body builder, but a grotesque and demonic version.

The thunder and lightning cracked through the skies. With his assailants close behind, James stopped dead in his tracks and turned around to face them. But they were gone.

He looked all around him, but there was no trace of them. It was just him, alone in the forest. The moment he let go and decided to face the demons, they disappeared. The harmonica music started again. James began to get a sense that this—whatever it was—was repeating itself over and over again.

Top Hat seemed like he was a richer, more refined man, while the large brute just looked overly muscular. James wasn't sure about the grim-looking girl in the wedding dress yet.

"Where are you, Tarif? It would seem that these demons torment you," James said aloud as he cautiously walked onward.

"Yes. They do."

James felt it, warm and sharp. The pain didn't set in right away, but as he hit the floor it came all in at once, splitting him in two.

"Aaargh!" He had been stabbed in the back. He reached around to feel for the knife and with all his strength he pulled it out. James rolled around on the floor in pain and looked up to see the girl in the wedding dress. She looked at him with disdain, smirking at her handy-work.

"Why? Why did you stab me?"

"You would ask me such a question? Humph." She turned around in defiance. James regained his strength and rose to his feet. Even though this dimension seemed to be affecting his abilities, he was still able to heal rapidly. James could see Top Hat in front of him, head cocked to one side, smiling while he spun his machete.

"You're the one in charge, aren't you, Top Hat? What's this about?"

"Isn't it obvious?" His voice made a screeching sound as he spoke.

"What have you done with Tarif? Who are you?"

"I'm the image, I'm the metaphor. When I'm around, what's wrong is right, and right is wrong. I am the answer to all life's problems! This is what he gave his life for." He opened his mouth, revealing thousands of jagged teeth. He lunged at James, taking a swipe towards his chest, nearly missing as James yielded backwards. He returned with a three punch combination to Top Hat's core, causing him to stumble back slightly. He lunged again, swiping furiously. James dodged and moved as fast as possible, staying slightly out of range.

"Tarif didn't give his life for you or anything like you. You're a monster." James came in with a series of kicks and punches, barely knocking him back. He absorbed James's blows with relative ease. Top Hat slammed the butt of his machete into James's face, followed by a slice to his shoulder. James stumbled backwards, right into the brute that followed them around. He grabbed James off him feet and threw him across the forest with all his strength. He flew over Top Hat and into a bank of trees.

For a moment there was only darkness, then James's sight came back as he saw them all running at him at full tilt. He quickly rose to his feet, jumping into the air, avoiding their attack. There was a nearby house, and James ran towards it as fast as he could. He could hear his attackers growling behind him. *Where was Tarif?* James had no way to escape in this dimension, but either way he wasn't leaving without Tarif. He was suffering in this hell and James was the only one who could save him now.

He made it to the house, and as he moved inside he noticed that there were dimly lit rooms within. There was not much room in there to fight with, but that was what James was hoping for. In a scramble, tight quarters might be to his advantage. They were strong, but not too smart. He also needed a break and a few moments to recover.

*Here they come.*

James ran upstairs and scaled a broken staircase up to the top floor as quickly as possible. They came in slowly and methodically, resembling some sort of psychotic kill squad. *What gives power to these illusions? Could it be Luzige?*

"Come on out, James. We know you're hiding. Why not come out and play? Remember when I said I was a metaphor? You didn't ask me for what. I am what Tarif always wanted to become, but the problem was there was no end to it. There was just never enough. Never satisfied." He clenched his massive jaws, his teeth grinding into position.

"There's always enough." James stepped out towards the banister at the top of the staircase. Top Hat glared at James with empty eyes, smiling a sickly vicious grin.

"Enough money? Of course not. That's why those who know how to acquire it simply horde it. It must be centralized, manipulated, controlled, and kept away from the huddled masses of undeserving peasants." He moved towards the staircase, walking methodically and slowly, keeping his eyes fixated on James. The brute and the girl in the wedding dress followed behind. James braced himself, then lunged forward with a flying kick from the top of the stairs, knocking them back down just enough to grab the machete out of Top Hat's hands. He leapt backwards up the staircase and flipped to his feet.

The brute came at him with tremendous force, swinging hay-maker punches. The sound of wind displacement could be heard as he unleashed a shower of strikes. Running up the wall, James leapt off with a slash, slicing open the brute's throat.

"That's where you're wrong. Anything centralized is subject to manipulation and control. Money is not something to be horded. It only works when it flows and is exchanged from hand to hand, that's how the economy works. When all the money is held by a wealthy few, all economy stops. Wealthy is also a perspective. Money as a 'thing' should only be valued when it enables an experience of growth. What you are is a grotesque depiction of everything money should never become."

"You are a fool. My kind and I are fuelled by the ignorance of billions. Wealth will never be decentralized. We will never meet the basic needs of man, and this is by design. Wealth can only exist if someone suffers." James looked as the muscled brute fell to the ground, unconscious, perhaps from loss of blood.

"And what about that monster over there, what's he supposed to be, Top Hat?"

"His name was Ruckus, for obvious reasons. He is the image longed for by many but with a little twist, of course. Many a monster does jealousy make. He doesn't speak for himself. I speak for him. Well, I did before you sliced his neck open. Not sure if he'll recover from that one."

"Where is Tarif? What have you done with him? He doesn't deserve this torment, he's suffered enough."

"That is not for you to decide, James."

"Then who decides?"

"Why, Tarif decides that, of course. You are so foolish; don't you see what's going on here? Everyone in the realm of Luzige tortures themselves. This is not about some force keeping us here. Luzige created these sub-realms so we might face our greatest enemies. This realm amplifies our deepest hatred, guilt, shame and fear. There is no escape because we can never escape ourselves. We will suffer here for all of time."

"No, that can't be."

"All of your friends will share the same fate. Luzige will feast on their souls, especially your precious Tamara."

"No!" James lashed forward with the machete, cutting Top Hat across the chest. He continued with a series of repeated slashes to his midsection.

"Leave him alone!" the girl in the wedding dress cried from the corner, but that didn't stop James from slashing him down, ending this once and for all.

"Now listen to me, Top Hat, these people might have chosen these circumstances, they may have created these hellish places, but that doesn't mean they're beyond saving. Luzige pushes them over the edge; he tempts the suicidal with a gun. But that doesn't mean they're beyond saving. That's where you're wrong."

"Life is a game of numbers. And the number of depressed and uninspired people is huge. They have been kept down too long, and their wings have been clipped. Luzige simply set a match to a world ready to ignite. We set the conditions for him to arrive; we allowed the power to be taken from us by the corrupted hearts of man. And now we pay the consequence."

"It's more than numbers; it's about the human desire for something greater. No matter how hard you try to suppress it, you cannot hold it back because it's the essence of what we are...to be more. Regardless of the past, regardless of what's been done, we can always strive to do better. At our core, we work to be better. There is more inside us than you give credit."

"Why not talk to me for a while, James?" The girl in the wedding dress spoke, the one who stabbed him. "How does your back feel?"

"Feels fine, thanks. What are you supposed to be?"

"I'm The Bride. I'm pretty, don't you think?"

"Not for my liking, sorry."

"I have a secret; do you care to know what it is?"

"I'm all ears."

"He's not really here, your friend."

"What are you talking about? Where is he?"

"Oh, he's around. He's just not here."

"You're not making any sense."

"You won't find him. He cannot be found."

"Is he the Grey Man I saw out there? What have you done with him?"

"Oh him, don't bother with him; he's not important. He's just a weak old fool wandering about, very harmless. Insecure, really. I don't even know if he knows how scared he is. He just keeps running. Never looks back, too scared to look. But I understand. I feel for him, I really do. We're all so fragile inside. We're so scared of life and of making the wrong choices."

"What the hell are you talking about?" James could see Top Hat out of the corner of his eye. He was getting back up on his feet.

"We're all very frightening, we are the dreams that never leave you. Sometimes people are scared of making their dreams real. It's too much responsibility, too much work, too much time, too much money, kids to take care of, and they are getting old, after all. Too late to make our dreams come true, right? So many broken promises, so many shattered dreams."

"Something tells me you never made it to your wedding." The nails on her hands grew longer, snapping out like knives. She screamed, slashing at him with all of her might. James yielded, circling around and delivered a straight pushing back kick to Top Hat, impaling him on splintered woods.

"You killed them! Aaargh!" She lunged at him, but James delivered a series of punches to her sternum and back. She spun around, slicing him across the face with both hands. She laughed as his blood spilled to the floor.

He stood up, healing from her blow. "Are you the wife Tarif could have had, or something? Cause if so, I'm happy he left you at the altar."

"No one left me, James. I never made it to the altar. I've been locked away where no one will find me. What I am is lost and the pain within will only multiply as each day passes. I am the unfulfilled promise." She moved closer to him, slithering like some sort of undead snake. She wasn't going down easily.

James looked up and saw the edge of the railing from the floor above. He jumped off a nearby table and grabbed the edge, losing the machete in the process. The girl reached for it, slashing away at his feet. James leaped up to the second floor, and made his way to the attic. There was an opening, and he climbed through and emerged onto the roof. The rain was pouring down as a steady stream of lightning flashed all around them. There had to be another way. He looked into the bushes behind the house, and there he was, the Grey Man. James scaled down the side of the house and ran over to him. "You know what this is about, don't you?"

He looked up at James and nodded. He looked vaguely like Tarif.

"Where is Tarif? I need your help, can you help me?"

He shook his head. "Who is Tarif? Who are you?"

"I'm his friend. I'm here to help him. He needs to leave this place. It's not safe here."

"Friend? You're his friend?"

"Yes, I'm his friend. I need to find him, can you help me? What do I need to do?"

"No. No, I can't help you. I can't face them."

"You have to try. Listen to me! Tell me where he is. How can I find Tarif?"

"Tarif?"

"Yes, Tarif. I'm his friend; I'm here to bring him home."

He looked up at James with a determined brow. "Okay, let's go home." He stood up with resolve, but was greeted with a stab through his heart.

"No!" James screamed as the Grey Man fell to the ground.

"Why do you want to know about him? He's just a facade. The hollow shell of a man and an empty insecure ego, nothing more."

"Yeah, well, he was my ticket to find Tarif and get the hell out of this place because clearly all of this mess has to do with you four. Now where is he? Is this his house? Where's Tarif?" He walked up to her and grabbed her dress by the straps. "Answer me! I'm done playing around."

"So am I!" She spun around, whipping her knife towards him, catching his right side which brought him to the ground. He quickly rolled out, but she followed close behind. He created scissors with his legs, bringing her down hard.

"There's only one way this ends. Finish this, or I'll finish you." He stared right into her eyes, and realized what needed to be done. He continued to roll forward towards her neck and snapped it.

As James stood up, all of his assailants began to disappear into a burst of light, which then gathered in the middle of the room. The energy formed into a single burst, as bright as a star until it took the shape of a man. The light dimmed until James could see him take shape. It was Tarif.

"Jacob! You're here!"

"Tarif! I can't believe it's you."

"It's me. How did you find me here? I remember the car crash and a few things after that. I was still alive after the crash. I mean I was dead, but I was still alive. I was standing outside of the car, watching everything. There were two men who worked for Netex. They were the ones who drove me off the road that night."

"I didn't know that was going to happen, Tarif; I should have never involved you. The Auditum Headset was my responsibility, not yours."

"You're my friend, Jake, and I tried to help you. Remember how much you helped me back in school? We were inseparable, you and I."

"You didn't deserve to be tortured like that. What happened to you? Do you remember?"

"Oh yes, I remember. After the car crash, my essence was floating over my body. I was watching the two men from Netex. They looked like security services. They said something about me now being out of the way, and now they'd have to go after Jacob. I became very detached from the scene, but also very curious and confused. I suddenly found myself in tremendous pain, as if I was being stabbed a thousand times all over my body. All around me was smoke, brimstone, and ash. Pillars of volcanic lava were shooting everywhere. That's when I saw Luzige."

"What did he say? What happened?"

"He said that it was time to embrace the inevitable. His forces were spilling into the Earth Realm, and soon he would be unleashed. He said that I was weak and incapable of comprehending the magnitude of what I was involved in. To prevent me from interfering and contacting you, Luzige fragmented me into different entities that were each a twisted outgrowth of my worst fears. Each of those entities was a part of me, the parts I never accepted. That is, until now. You reminded me that there is always hope, always another chance to do better. After you defeated me, I forgave myself."

"Then you became whole again."

"Acceptance is about forgiving and loving yourself. You gave me an opportunity to confront my beliefs and release myself from my nightmare."

"There's more you're not telling me, isn't there."

"Yes. That night, I found a file on Edward Aidan's computer that was worse than anything I could have imagined. Project Auditum was a covert military test bed for mind control technology. There were six other trials of Auditum technology, and you were the seventh."

"They were testing it on me?"

"And they were drugging you. They were experimenting with a Pituitary gland stimulator, which caused tumours in the brain that could be directly controlled through Auditum."

"So they drugged me?"

"Yes. Using the drug and the headset, they could control a subject or kill them on a whim. But there were oddities in the trials; some didn't take to the drug. It affected them differently, causing their brain to increase in capacity and function. I believe that's what happened to you, Jake."

"That's why all of those experiences were happening to me. That's why I could see energy and hear people's thoughts."

"And travel to different dimensions, yes. That's what you're doing right now."

"But now it's different. I'm different. I'm in a different body, I look different and I..."

"You are still Jacob. Once you became a being of light, you transcended the physical plane and entered the Summerlands. This is where we typically come from, and go to after a physical life is complete. It's simply a realm where beings of a certain level of consciousness live, and a place many of us call home. That's where we incarnate from. That's where you got your new body."

"How do you know?"

"Because I can feel it. I'm being called home. It's finally time for me to rest awhile."

"You deserve it, my friend. Go find peace in the Summerlands."

"There's something else. You have to find Tamara. He's taken her and if he has her much longer, she will lose all memory of you. She loves you, Jake, and she's trying to hold on, but you need to find her."

"Where is she? I dream of her all the time. I do love her."

"He's taken her to the Priory of Despair, his lowest realm. Find her before it's too late."

"Thanks, Tarif."

"Just focus. Remember her. You'll find her."

# SEVENTEEN

## AN UNLIKELY HERO

J AMES WOKE TO the sounds of clashing and shattered glass as
the car slammed through a bank of bushes and trees. "What's going
on? Where are we?"

"We almost got killed about three times since you fell asleep, that's
what's going on. Thanks for joining us!" Sarah screamed as the car
continued to crash through some bushes. The engine gave out as it
rolled into a nearby city street.

"This isn't good." Joshua exclaimed.

"What's going on?"

"Listen, James. In about ten seconds, we're going to be surrounded
by a band of marauders that hunts people for sport. If they catch us, we're
dead. Grab everything and run!"

It took James a moment to digested, but then started to grab
everything around him, including the Auditum headset, and ran towards
Sarah who was already out of the car. Joshua grabbed his weapons and
limped over to them, still wincing from his stab wound.

They took momentary refuge from their pursuers behind some
abandoned cars in the street. James was still clearing his head, recovering

from using Auditum. "You're hurt," he said, motioning towards Josh's injury.

"It's only a flesh wound; I'll live. What happened when you were under? Was it worth it?"

"Yeah. I think it was. I helped an old friend, and he told me how to find her. Tamara."

"But what about Luzige? Can we stop him?"

"I don't know yet. I think so"

"What do you mean you don't know?" Just then a grenade bounced off the wall and landed right beside them. Josh quickly grabbed it and threw it over the bank of cars.

Josh ducked down, grabbing Sarah and James just as the grenade exploded. What followed was a laugh bellowing through the trees.

"They've found us! Quick, through the alley!" Josh whispered.

"How much ammo do we have?"

"We've got nothing left. We gave them everything we had when they tried to run us off the road. You were asleep for that one."

"Sorry, but it was worth it. I think there's a way to get Luzige out of our dimension for good."

"None of that will matter if we die here. There are at least fifteen of these guys, and they're heavily armed and wearing body armour. They look like ex-military, and they aren't playing around. We need to find cover and wait them out. We don't stand a chance taking them head on."

"Yes, you're right. Let's duck inside that old computer shop." They rallied Sarah and quietly made their way into the store. James felt edgy and kept peeking out the window.

"Josh, are we going to be okay in here?" Sarah asked sheepishly.

"Quiet, someone's coming." James looked out the window and saw two large men approaching dressed in military fatigues. They stared down the scopes of their rifles as they patrolled the street, passing right by the computer shop. "Okay, they're gone. We've got to move."

"Agreed. Let's see if this place has a back exit." The three of them moved to the back of the store. The fire escape door was down a flight of steps. They moved out, single file, into the back alley behind the building.

They walked a few yards before two marauders came from behind them, pulling back their gun triggers.

"Well, well, what do we have here?" Their muffled voices could be heard through their military-issue environment breathers.

"Looks like a few people who missed curfew, doesn't it? That's going to cost you, big time." They moved in, guns pointed and ready to fire. Shots suddenly rang out from above, taking the marauders by surprise and connecting with them both squarely in the forehead.

A woman dropped out from the trees, holding a gun. "My name's Nancy Moretti. You folks had better follow me. There's a set of stairs that leads up here, let's go. There isn't much time before the rest of them get here." James, Josh, and Sarah all ran towards Moretti, who then motioned them to follow her to a back room. "In the closet there's a hidden entrance." Sarah looked sceptical, but followed in desperation.

"Trust me, this is the only way," Moretti said. They followed her into the closet, which had a gaping hole in the back, revealing a dark pathway through the drywall. They went in, being extremely careful not to create any creeks in their stepping. The sounds of the army marauders could be heard through the walls. They were viciously describing what they would do if they'd found them.

They made it through the walls, and out to another room, which led to a window and fire escape. They walked along, scaling the wall and trying to avoid making shadows. James was the last one to exit via the window, as the rest made their way down the fire escape.

"Hey! Not so fast."

James turned around to see a rather large marauder standing in the doorway. "Leaving so soon? I thought you wanted to play." The marauder dropped his gun, and walked very quickly towards James, releasing a strike to his face, knocking him to the floor. The marauder jumped on top of him, continuing to grab and pummel James. "Hey, what's the deal, not interested in fighting?"

"Oh I am, but I just wanted to give my friends enough time to escape. Now we can play." James rolled onto his feet and swept the marauder's leg out from under him, sending him back onto the floor.

"Nice trick." The marauder said, struggling back to his feet, which was not an easy task with so much body armour.

"I've got lots of them." The man charged at him with a hay-maker. Easily yielded by James, he moved to the side and readied a parrying position. As the marine released his strike, James quickly evaded it while deflecting his opponent's arm, tossing it aside, and releasing his own strike squarely to the marauder's forehead.

"Hmm, you're pretty fast, kid."

"No, you're just making me look good," James replied. The marauder chuckled under his breath as he rose to his feet once more charging with a knee, and combination of strikes, all easily evaded by James.

"You know, getting angrier is not going to help you."

Wheezing, the marine rested against the wall. "Oh yeah? We'll see." Raging towards him, the ex-marine released a combination of strikes that nearly connected, but were easily blocked and retaliated against.

"So, smart-ass. What am I doing wrong?" Again, he charged at James with his last reserves of energy, flying towards him with a drop kick. James shoved and redirected him in mid-air, sending him hurling and screaming out the window to his death several stories below.

"Telegraphing your strikes."

James finally caught up to Moretti, Sarah, and Josh up the street. Nancy Moretti was a name that James still remembered from his previous life. Vague recollections of her documenting what happened to Jacob raced through his brain; he remembered her recording his story, and helping him stay out of jail.

"If we stay off the main road we might have a chance," Moretti told them.

"Where are you taking us?" James asked.

"Somewhere safe. Those men are the Merchant Marauders. Ex-military, or otherwise highly trained, some as high as CIA or even KIA, the Government's psychic forces. They banded together after the government collapsed. They were trained to survive, and that's what they do, except they also feed off of the fear and desperation of others. How did they find you?"

"They found us driving along the road after dark. We were on our way back to the main city when they drove us off the road. We slammed into a bank of trees, and then made out on foot. That's basically when you found us. Thanks for your help." Joshua said, clutching his side and breathing hard.

"You're hurt. We need to get that looked after right away. Did one of those guys get you?"

"No, it was something else, a mutant of some kind. It slashed me and got me pretty good, actually. I should be fine, but yes, sooner rather than later I'm going to need some attention." James stared curiously at the wound, saying nothing. He listened to them speaking, but he was in another world, reliving the experiences in the dream world, the Summerland, and all the other realms he's visited. He wondered why it was so different there. Whereas there you can heal by the touch of your hand and complete belief, here you had to rely on time to heal.

James shook his head and snapped back to the present. "We need to move. They're coming."

Sarah grabbed her things and helped Joshua to his feet.

"The only place we can go where these guys won't think about going is deep into the inner city," Moretti said.

"Are you kidding? There's a reason they won't go there: it's overrun by mutants!" Sarah whispered loudly.

"We're dead either way. If we stay on the main road, they will just kill us off one by one. If we go into the forest, they will hunt us down. Our only chance is to go where they don't want to go."

"And how come you have become the leader of our group all of a sudden? What makes you an expert?" Sarah asked.

"Because she used to be a cop. She was part of the Toronto division turned freelancing mercenary. Is that about right?" James cut into the conversation.

"You're pretty close. I'm also an expert because I used to be one of those bastards. They recruited much of the police force, RCMP, and whoever else they could. They amassed weapons and resources so quickly that people joined them in waves. So yes, I was one of those marauders, so I know how they think and what they're after."

"I can only imagine why you left them." Sarah said quietly.

"Yeah, well, I was with them for a few years, but once I saw how they treated the people they captured so I got the hell out of there. I was slowly becoming a target anyway, so I was better off on my own."

"They just let you leave?" Sarah asked.

"Let's just say I had to make a very explosive exit. But more importantly," she said as she looked at James, "how the hell do you know who I am? You look a little like Jacob Cross, but that's impossible. He's dead."

"I am Jacob Cross. And you're right, I did die, but now I'm back. I can't explain how or why exactly, but I've returned to this dimension and I'm trying to stop Luzige."

"And you're all following this guy?" she said as she looked at the group.

They nodded.

"So you're all crazy, in other words." She shook her head in disbelief. "Okay, come with me." Moretti readied her pistol and briskly made it across the court yard with the others in lockstep. She continued until the buildings around them became more and more dilapidated, looking less like houses and more like ruins.

Wrestling in the shadows could be seen and heard as they approached the inner city and the horrors that awaited them. As the group walked onwards, there was heaviness in the air, and they thought about how they may have simply traded one problem for another.

"No sign of the merchant marines, Moretti. I think we need to rest for a moment." Josh stated.

"There's a medical supply store close by and some old pharmacies. There might be something in there to bandage you up."

They arrived at an abandoned pharmacy, which had obviously been broken into several times. "Let's all go in there together," Sarah said, looking wide-eyed at her surroundings and biting her lip. They slowly walked through the broken window and looked for bandages or basic first aid materials. Sarah found a needle and thread and some rubbing alcohol. Nancy found bandages, and they sat down to patch up Joshua.

"I'll be right back; I'm going to check out the storage room." James cautiously moved to the rear of the store through a narrow hallway that led to the storage area. Thinking that there might be some other useful materials in the room, he continued farther, not realizing a creature stalking his every move, scaling the ceiling above him. As James stopped, the creature stopped. Perfectly silent and in harmony with his every move, the dark stalker was only visible by the reflections of its eyes.

James could feel he was not alone, but fought against the sensation as he moved into the storage area and searched through a couple of boxes. Finding only wrappers and empty packages, he kept moving. In the distance, a pile of cartons and large boxes were barely able to hide the movement of several more creatures, now alerted to his presence. James, ever cautious, looked all around him and noticed the walls were alive with humanoid creatures. Their movement was snake-like, agile and silent. They all began opening their eyes, revealing hundreds.

James could feel the shift in the air as they began turning towards him, ready to attack. In the same moment, he could feel their apprehension and tension as they all braced for a feeding frenzy. At once, James let go of himself and let the circumstances dictate his actions. He knew a fight was inevitable, but how quickly and how viciously it ended would be up to them.

They lunged at him simultaneously and, as if in slow motion, James responded with a series of throws, yields, and continuous strikes.

"Josh, Sarah, Moretti! RUN!" It was all James could yell before being toppled by several strikes from the hideous creatures. He emerged from the dog pile, trying to throw them off of him. Josh, Sarah, and Moretti came in the room, trying to shoot several that leaped towards them.

"What are they?" Sarah screamed in terror.

"They're Grimsers, a group of Catalyst infected natives. Because there's nothing left to eat, they are always starving; that's why they're so thin. Only the Catalyst keeps them alive. They are vicious, and they multiply like crazy. We've just walked right into their nest and they think we're lunch!"

"There has to be hundreds of them in there!" Josh shouted as he wrestled with about three or four of them. They were light weight, dark and broken-skinned mutants, but they had razor sharp teeth. James was still caught in the middle, and he struggled to fight his way back to his feet, throwing punches and snapping appendages in a seemingly non-stop fashion.

Sarah made her way out of the line of fire, looking for something useful. She stumbled onto a fire extinguisher and brought it back, unleashing it onto the pack of Grimsers. They all stumbled back, scattering like rats.

"Thanks, Sarah." James rose to his feet, stretching out his neck and back. All the Grimsers rallied back into a circular formation, ready to leap. James got back into a fighting stance. "Okay, let's try that again."

They all leaped at him simultaneously, but he was prepared this time with lightning speed, he began striking, parrying, and throwing everything in his reach. James disabled them with each strike, breaking bones with every contact, taking the Grimsers right out of the fight. Teeth flew, and the sound of bones snapping echoed across the room. Their numbers and volumes increased, but so did his response as his forearms and fists began glowing white hot.

"I knew it! I knew it was him!" Joshua exclaimed as James continued his flurry of strikes. All that could be seen was a white glow at the centre of the room completely obliterating anything that threatened to attack him. The Grimser numbers died down, and the remaining injured slinked away. The white hot light around James began to subside as he walked back towards Josh, Sarah, and Moretti. Steam rose off his body as the sheer heat of the energy being channelled was tremendous.

"Maybe you are Jacob Cross after all," Moretti admitted. "I haven't seen you in nearly seven years. You look different from what I remember. What happened to your eyes?"

"The man you knew is dead. Part of him is within me, but I'm something else entirely now," James said firmly. "Call me James."

"The last time I saw you, you were in a hospital bed, barely able to move. I remember talking to the doctors about your recovery time, and when I returned…your body was gone. You had vanished. We searched your apartment, asked your friends, and put out an all-points alert in order to track you down. But, we never found you." Said Moretti.

"The moments leading up to my transition are cloudy to me. I don't remember a lot from those days."

"Your technology has something to do with all of this, doesn't it?" Moretti interrupted.

"I'm afraid it does, but I didn't cause this. Edward Aidan used the technology, unleashing the monster you know as Luzige onto the world. I tried to stop it, but I was too weak at the time."

"I'm not sure how that's possible, or even why you're here. But I've only ever seen one other person do that and that's Lukman. Either you're him, or you've learned how to fight like he did." Sarah interjected.

"It's him," said Joshua.

# EIGHTEEN

## THE DEFILER

T HEY LEFT THE pharmacy and the den of Grimsers behind them and proceeded to the centre of town. The flashlights from the marauders could be seen in the distance, but they weren't following them this far into the city without heavy artillery. They pressed on until they found an abandoned house with missing windows and doors and just enough visibility and exits to be a useful rest stop.

"James, how were you able to light up like that?" Sarah asked as they settled down for the night.

"I think it has something to do with the Auditum headset. When I use it, it allows me to access powers from other dimensions. In my dreams, I'm able to fight like that, yet after using the headset, I'm able to fight like that here too."

"Auditum is bringing you more in line with your powers. Interesting." Joshua dropped his bags and laid down a blanket for them to rest on.

"I remember you talking about headsets when I first met you, when you were Jacob. That's what put you in the hospital to begin with, and now you're using it again?"

"It gets worse, Nancy; those headsets are what destroyed our world." Sarah interrupted.

"What are you talking about?" Moretti asked. "Luzige and his mutant mercenaries are what destroyed everything. He worked with the Arabe'en and coordinated a global terrorist attack."

"Yes, that's what everyone believes. They called it the fulfilment of the Arabe'en 'End Games Prophecy.' They also said that Luzige released the Catalyst into the water supply and caused this mutant apocalypse. Well, they're mostly right, but as usual, they're missing the whole picture." Joshua added.

"Just spit it out, already. What are you trying to say, Josh?"

"The government was working with a company called Netex. They corrupted the food and water supplies and injected the Catalyst mutagenic agent into everything. Auditum technology was reserved for the elites and controlled by Netex. The headset opened a gateway, allowing Luzige to pour into this dimension and possess the CEO of Netex, thus taking physical form. He's used the same headset to bring his other generals into our realm. He's turning our world into his own personal hell."

"What? Why is he doing this?"

"He is pure evil. I don't know how or why he was summoned, but he became aware of our world and has targeted us for annihilation. He's dismantled most governments around the world, as they're too busy dealing with the chaos of the mutant invasion."

"Yes, I've seen the rest with my own eyes. Towns have sprung up, but most innovation has stopped completely. We've devolved, turning back into savages. How can we stop this?"

"By stopping Luzige once and for all." James said firmly.

"And how do you suppose we'll do that?" Sarah asked.

"I have to go back."

"Where?" Moretti asked.

"Back into the other dimensions. I have to use Auditum again; there's something I have to do."

"You're going back for her, aren't you? For Tamara?"

"Yes, I am."

"But James, what does she have to do with any of this? You need to focus on the problem at hand. If we don't stop Luzige, we're dead. And even if we survive, what's there to live for? This world is a disaster. We can't find happiness under his tyranny."

"She's the key to all of this, I know it. He has her trapped, and I have to save her. That's the last thing that Tarif said to me before I released him from his prison. He told me I have to find her, and that's what I'm going to do. I need you guys to watch over me tonight. I don't know how long I'll be under."

"We've got your back." Josh said.

"Thank you." James settled down and made himself comfortable. He pulled the headset out of his backpack and looked at it for a moment. *It looks like one of the originals from Netex,* he thought to himself. But enough reminiscing. *It's time.*

He put it on, made a few quick adjustments, and turned it on. He closed his eyes and thought of Tamara, remembering her tenderness and how she always took care of him when they were together. He remembered her intently, just as Tarif told him to. Glimpses of her lifting a cup to his lips and helping him drink flashed through his mind. Images of training with Boulos in the other realms, and her, watching and helping.

He began recalling different times on the beach, meeting with her on several occasions. Vividly, he saw her in his mind, standing in front of him with the wind blowing gently around them. Then it all changed. Darkness began to roll in as clouds coated the sky. The once serene beach became a war zone of lightning and thunder, but she still stood there. She began fading before his eyes, and while he reached for her.

"Tamara, wait!" As he moved towards her, the world around him turned completely dark. He started falling faster and faster, completely out of control.

The air got thicker and hotter as he fell, until finally James broke through the ceiling of a gigantic stone structure, falling hundreds of feet to the floor. He crashed into the ground, causing a small crater that smelled of ash and brimstone.

James found himself in a large cavern that resembled the innards of a large cave. Metal and concrete mixed to create a very inhospitable terrain to tread through. Looking around, he didn't notice any other people or living things. The echoes of dripping water could be heard throughout the caves, and the place smelled of death. The occasional shriek of pain bellowed out of the shadows, as if a prolonged torturing was underway.

The lightness and suppleness of other realms were not with him here. He was more dense and slow. His awareness was also dampened, as he was quickly losing track of his objective.

*Think of Tamara, think of Tamara.* James thought, hoping to push off the effects of this dimensional amnesia. In the distance was a city with several pillars of smoke and ash spewing from various industrial stacks. It reminded James of an old part of Toronto, full of factories and pollution. As those are the only signs of life nearby, he headed there.

He remembered what Josh had said about Luzige and his generals. He didn't quite realize that there were other entities from Luzige's dimensions that had entered the earth realm. How many were there? He thought about his many questions as he made his way towards the city engulfed in flames.

As he approached, he could see pillars of ash and smoke billowing from the ground, causing fire to burst through the crevices of the earth. The only light that was visible was from the fiery pits, and burning ash forming clouds in the sky. The darkness and terror in the air were like a thick fog, leaving him unnerved as it touched him. He felt the trembling of tortured souls off in the distance. Barely visible, he could see packs of wild animals tearing into a corpse, while others were brutalized in different ways. This was a place of torture that much was certain.

James wondered how he'd find Tamara amongst all of this despair. He remembered what Tarif said and kept focusing on her. *Focus on the good things.* He envisioned her standing on the beach in her flowery dress. A magnificent beach surrounded her, with crystal blue crashing waves, a sapphire sky, and a bright, nourishing sun.

As difficult as it was, he held on to the image and pressed forward. The surrounding energy tried to seep into his soul and create doubts, insecurities, and fears. The image of Tamara became less clear as the beach turned red and the water black. The sky became dark purple, and Tamara's body was as cracked and burnt as the cave he walked through to find her. Her eyes turned to flames, her hair a dark crimson red, and her dress a longer, more tattered version of what it once was.

James broke from his vision as he approached a large bridge. He could see from a certain angle that there were people underneath it, huddled up and talking to each other. He moved closer in the hopes of catching a better glimpse. He saw a man dressed in tattered clothing, his hands wrapped in dirty bandages and his face obscured by a hat with a low brim. He was talking with a short, fat woman who was loud, poorly clothed, and chewing on something. There were quite a few of them under there, and at first glance they seemed approachable.

James moved in closer and said, "Hey, what is this place? I'm looking for someone, can you help me?" Several of them turned around, including the man with the bandages. A few in the background could be heard laughing at him. "I'm just asking for directions, can you help?" He approached in a cautious, friendly manor.

"Directions? To where?" the fat lady asked.

"I'm looking for my friend. I was told to focus on her, but I can't get a good reading in this place. Everything seems distorted here."

"Of course you can't get a good reading here: this place is a prison. No one leaves this place. It just corrupts you and consumes you. It makes you think of everything you've ever done badly, and multiplies it. It disconnects you and separates you. Only those who are condemned to suffer come here, and suffering is all you *can* do here. So I ask you again: directions to where? Where the hell do you think you're going?" James took a moment to recover from her explanation.

"Listen to me! Can any of you tell me how to find a woman? Her name is Tamara. She is trapped down here, and I need to find her."

"You think she's the only one trapped down here, bub? We're all trapped. Including you."

"No, I'm not like the rest of you, I'm only here because I'm using a technology called Auditum. It brought me here, and I can use it to leave when I'm ready."

The entire mob of vagrants under the bridge broke out into hysterical laughter.

"That's a new one. I thought I'd heard it all: *I'm special...I'm not supposed to be here...this is a mistake...*but now I've heard everything. *I'm only here because I used some technology, and I can leave whenever I want.*" The man in bandages erupted back into laughter along with the fat lady.

"Okay, this is useless; I'll find her on my own."

"Sorry, kid, but you're out of your mind. If you think you can leave, do it. I dare you. I want to watch you just poof and disappear like you said. Come on, kid, I'm waiting."

"I don't have time for this."

"Okay, okay I'm just messing with ya. If you really want to find your friend like you say, here's what you do. Anything that's even close to sweet and innocent in this city gets immediately taken to the iron foundry, to the pit. That's so they can torture any last bit of hope out of you. All you have to do is follow the heat. The hotter it gets, the closer you are. It's through the bridge. Just follow the path and you'll get there. But don't forget, this place will play tricks on you. You'll see things from your past that aren't really there. Don't get caught up in the illusions."

"Thank you. Can I ask you a question?"

"Sure. You made me laugh, I owe you."

"Why are you down here anyway? What happened to you?"

"Arson." He began to unwrap the bandages around his hands and body, revealing charred and mangled skin, burnt away to almost nothing. He began laughing again, this time at the shock on James's face. James pressed onwards, through the bridge, and onto the path pointed out by the man in bandages.

The cityscape burned as he followed the path. The journey certainly became longer and hotter as he went on. The path turned metallic and it burnt James's feet as he walked over it. Doing what he could to avoid it, he still felt incredibly vulnerable in this dimension. He thought of what the man had said, that this realm was only for those condemned to suffer, and that this place forces you to relive your past.

Perhaps James was lucky that he could barely remember his past. He felt less burdened than the people he met under the bridge, but what about Tamara? What burdens did she bear, and how did this dimension corrupt her? James wasn't sure that Tamara was consumed by the sheer evil in this dimension, but the visions he conjured of her in his mind lacked the beauty and strength they once had. Instead, as he remembered her, the visions themselves festered and boiled, turning her into a tortured version of what she once was.

Either way, he remembered Tarif's advice: keep remembering her. Remember her how she once was. Remember the good times, and the love they had shared. Even though James's path became scalding hot, the vision he had in his mind distracted him from the terrain. He focused unrelentingly on a positive portrait of her in his mind, as if flexing a muscle, not allowing the forces of the dimension to corrupt the image.

He stumbled as he walked on the path, realizing there was a massive pit only footsteps away. This broke his concentration, and all at once, as if a flood came rushing into his mind, the pristine image of her became instantly consumed by evil. *There are evil forces at work here.* He feared that he may not be powerful enough to stop them.

He also remembered that one of the characteristics of this realm was to magnify doubts, insecurities, and fears. Better to not think of doubts at all. The pit below smelled like brimstone and burning bodies. It was a large gaping hole in the grown with stairs carved from stone that spiralled down to the heart of the pit.

Journeying onwards, he could feel the sheer heat billowing from the clouds of steam and ash. Rivers of molten lava and flames circulated below him as the surface world got farther and farther away. Walking for what seemed like hours, James arrived close to the bottom, where tremors rippled through the ground and a horrific river of bodies, blood, and molten rock flowed in all directions. Looking up and around, James noticed the rivers flowed into a large cavern which stood hundreds of feet tall.

Making his way into the cavern, the tremors got stronger, as did the smell of death and ash. He was getting closer, but to what exactly, he wasn't sure. Rounding a corner, he realized the purpose of the river, the tremors, and the smelting of human souls. There, standing nearly five hundred feet tall, stood a mammoth creature, part spider and part human. It looked to be made of mostly burnt flesh, stone, and metal, and as it walked across the cavern at incredible speed, it produced smoke and tremors that shook the entire pit.

This creature somehow fed off of the river of souls, scooping people up and chewing on them, giving them little time to suffer and screech in agony before being completely consumed. *Is this what happened to Tamara? Did this monster devour her like he has all the rest of these poor souls?*

He had to stop thinking that way and focus on the matter at hand. This gigantic creature must be one of Luzige's generals for this realm. The creature was too busy consuming souls to notice James slowly moving against the wall, trying to gain a different viewpoint. On a level about ten stories above him, there was a series of cages built into the wall. James managed to get back on the stairs without being seen by the hulking spider guardian. He looked in each one of the cages; some were empty, and others were not. Some were filled with people, naked, and in various stages of being eaten alive. They screamed at him as he walked by. "Let us out! Please let us out!"

"If I let you out, that thing will just see you and eat you right away."

"Please, don't leave us like this!"

He thought for a moment "Okay, but you all have to be really quiet and stop moaning, for God's sake. Follow the stairs all the way up and out of this pit. It will take you a long time, but just keep moving, you'll get out of here eventually. Now go!" He unchained the door. It was poorly locked, but they were too weak to even open it themselves.

Many whispered their thanks to him as at least thirty people walked out of their cages. James pressed forward, looking cage by cage, trying to find her. There were at least a hundred cages, but that didn't stop him. Most were empty; some were filled with angry animals or defiled people. James helped who he could as he checked each cage. He thought to himself for a moment, about judgement and retribution. Like the man under the bridge who suffered burnt hands and arms due to his life of arson, Luzige feasted on him and his need to pay for his crimes. Did these people also have crimes they were punishing themselves for? He thought of his time in the Summerlands and his talks with Orion. In that place, there was no judgement, and people felt the warmth of a loving force, a creator, wherever they went. Why was that void here? *They lack awareness*, he thought as he pressed forward.

A woman in tattered clothing came to up Jacob and thanked him with a kiss on the cheek. "You've saved what's left of my soul. I thought all hope was lost."

"What is that thing?"

"It's called *The Defiler*, and you're in his iron foundry. Who are you, and how did you get here?" She asked him.

"My name is James, and I'm here looking for someone. A woman named Tamara."

"I see."

"And you are?"

"My name is Christie. You know, this used to be a beautiful place. My world. Until all of these creatures arrived."

"What do you mean? What is this place? Where are we?"

"You're on Earth of course."

"Earth! How can this be Earth? I thought this was some level of hell."

"Well, poetically, you're not far off. This place has been turned into this hell by these creatures."

"How can this be? I'm only visiting here using a technology from my own world, my own version of Earth." It was beginning to slowly make sense to him.

"Your own version of Earth?"

"I have a physical body on my own planet. Using the Auditum

Technology, a headset that I developed, I've travelled to different dimensions and this is one of them."

"Well, everything here is pretty physical also."

His gut twisted as he thought of something. "Christie, this must be some kind of parallel Earth reality that I've come to. Others have called this place the Realm of Despair… I thought I was entering some kind of dimension of hell."

"People have called this place by that name. And you have entered a dimension of hell, figuratively."

"No, no." Jacob shook his head, feeling dizzy. He began to realize the truth behind the Auditum technology. It was more than something allowing him to have out-of-body experiences and travel to different dimensions. It was bridging him completely between realities. What he thought was some astral realm of hell was actually a tormented and twisted version of Earth, one with monstrous entities walking the planet and destroying all in their path. People of all places and times were devoured and their fear was fed off of. This place was the calling card of Luzige.

"There's only one last place to look for your friend." Christie said, still grateful for being set free. "You have to look for her in a place called The Caldron. That's where the people of Earth who do not adhere and obey go to be tortured and killed, in the most vial of ways. If she's here, that's where they'd keep her."

"Where can I find this place?"

"The river of fire and molten rock below, which is what the Defiler feasts on, leads directly to The Caldron. You have to get past him, follow the river, and you'll find her."

Some of the escaped prisoners who had walked ahead started tripping over themselves and making noises. They pushed over a rock, which fell several stories, landing next to the gargantuan beast below. The people on the stairs froze in horror as the rock made a loud noise and alerted the creature. In a slow movement that sounded like the twisting of metal, the creature moved its body and looked up, noticing their attempted escape.

With demonic speed, it began scaling the walls and smashing through rock and steel to get to them. It climbed the tunnel like a large spider after its prey. With haste it began grabbing and eating any human it could find. Climbing up faster and faster, searching through empty cages, the creature was angry that its food source was walking away. James and a cloister of people hid in a small alcove as they watched the creature devouring others before their eyes.

"You have to do something!" someone screamed.

The screams of the deathly opera continued as the remorseless demon grabbed at everyone James had saved, except for a last few. Determined to save the people, James took command of the situation.

"Wait here." He motioned forward slightly, peering out to get a better angle, and noticed the creature just below him, attached to the wall using its large legs and fangs, searching for whatever it could find. There was no other way to escape. James had to do something to stop this horrendous creature.

The Defiler moved with incredible swiftness for a being of its size, but James knew it must have a weakness. He looked around and saw a bed of jagged rocks far below them. He slowly moved out to position himself near the stairs which were far above the bed of stone spikes.

"Hey, over here, you freak!"

All at once, the creature jumped and grappled the rocks near James's position, climbing up on its hind legs, revealing several rows of monstrous fangs as it moved in for its kill. James got up and ran as quickly as he could across the stairs, up and over as many rocks and through as many cages as possible. The monster ran after him with lightning agility and reflexes, destroying everything in its wake until he ran and slid under a short gap between two large boulders. The creature smashed into the wall, and nearly toppled James. Pinning him to the ground, The Defiler took only an instant to try and tear him apart with a final strike.

James used all of his focus and raised his hands in protection. Around him formed a large purple and white portal of energy, a dimensional tear, coming directly from his palms and large enough to consume the beast. As this occurred, The Defiler disappeared, then reappeared in mid-air and fell towards the lava pit below. People started shouting behind him.

"How did you do that?"

"He created some kind of portal!"

As it fell, it made one last attempt to latch onto the sides of the wall, but lost its footing. It slipped backward and screeched in terror as it fell thousands of feet towards the pointed rocks surrounded by molten lava. It was instantly impaled, and sunk towards the depths of the iron foundry into a fiery death. The remaining people came out of the walls and cheered for James, but he couldn't rejoice with them for very long, as he realized there was still work to be done.

# NINETEEN

## RIVER OF FIRE

JAMES WALKED THE path along the river of fire, feeling the temperatures rise and the lights become brighter as he journeyed forward. The air became thick and smelled of ash and sulphur. The river contained the tattered remains of people and things, all destroyed by the destruction of the Earth realm. And Auditum might just be the cause of all of it. James thought that somehow he had been the cause that enabled Luzige to enter their world, and take over. And it wasn't just happening in James's version, it was happening in parallel universes across creation. Using Auditum, Jacob Cross opened the door and Luzige walked right through it.

How many realities had Luzige destroyed? And how many times had Jacob helped him do it? He thought about this as he walked towards The Caldron. James refocused and centred himself. Only by focusing inwardly could he come up with the clarity of mind to resolve all of this and determine a next step. He focused and cleared his mind as visions of Tamara's face appeared. Her eyes and hair were made of pure fire, and her skin was white hot, with veins visible like finely linked chains. Her presence was immense as she flowed with a kind of power James hadn't seen before. Her body was made of fiery skin, and her dress could barely contain the sheer force of her energy.

James snapped out of the vision and gave his head a shake. She must be becoming more corrupted by Luzige's presence, and time was running out. He ran with all of his might down the tunnel, feeling the heat increase with each step as he got closer.

He flew forward at an incredible speed until he reached a giant basin where all rivers of fire poured into a set of machines that was somehow fuelled by the lava. This contraption generated power for the systems and tunnels connected to it. The river flowed into an inconceivable inferno that was in the centre of the room, upon which there was a giant platform with controls and other unfamiliar machines. Intricate stone staircases connected all parts of the massive room.

The air was hot and thick, and all around him were sets of copper steam pipes with elaborate carvings upon them. They connected together at various points, and they all had something to do with keeping The Caldron working.

He proceeded slowly as there was no one in sight, but as he moved deeper, he could feel a set of eyes watching him. There was a constant hissing sound in the room as the steel melted and steam rose to the connecting piping systems. The sounds of opening and closing valves could also be heard, then a few moments of silence, and then the sounds began again. James walked further into the room, and the pipes becoming more maze-like with various twists and turns leading towards the room's centre.

As he journeyed into the middle of this massive auditorium, he realized that he must be within the Engine room. The twists and turns became too numerous to keep track of, and even all the pipes, as intricate as they were, began to look the same. He was lost.

The air was damp and hot. Fifty or so Grimsers came out of nowhere and began to chase him. He ran through the pipes and corridors, with only the light of the fires around them to provide sight. Racing through and sliding over pipes, James could barely stay ahead of the Grimsers, who seemed to increase in numbers as they chased him at top speed.

James finally made it into a large clearing. Near the centre was a large chasm, and as he ran towards it, so did the hundreds of Grimsers. Without hesitation he jumped as far and high as he could into the lava pit, with all of the Grimsers following behind him.

Before James along with the Grimsers could fall to their deaths, a hand grabbed him out of nowhere. The hand that grabbed him was hot and felt scaly. It was hard like stone, but smaller, that of a woman's hand. As James saw the hundreds of Grimsers tumbling like lemmings beneath him, he looked up to see who had saved him.

"Tamara!" A memory of what she once was hovered over the lava pit, holding James above certain death. But her beauty was now corrupted and demonic. Her power was overwhelming as she levitated in a dark aura, suspending both herself and James in mid-air. Their eyes caught each other's, but before any form of remembrance could occur, she tossed him across the room onto a bed of pipes.

She flew at him with incredible force and speed, and tackled him like a missile, sending him flying across the room once more. She walked towards him again, and then picked up the pace, grabbing his face and smashing it into her knee. She grabbed him by the hair, and smashed his face repeatedly with her fist, throwing him to the ground.

James did little to retaliate, too overwhelmed to think straight. She walked up to him again, relentless in her attack.

Grabbing him by the throat, she began to glow a fierce red colour as she punched him with bone-crushing force. She was incredibly strong, and he could barely maintain consciousness throughout the onslaught. Within seconds, Tamara had completely toppled him.

He was barely able to stand as she completely drained what was left of his energy.

"James, are you leaving me so soon? We were just about to have some fun!"

"T-t-amara…" She picked him up by the hair, lifting him to his feet.

"Now listen to me. You can't stop any of this, it's already been done. Just as it is in this world. My *home world*. So too will it be in yours, very soon. You see, Luzige is all powerful. He has corrupted everything he touches, and with each defiling, he grows stronger. He will corrupt all creation if not stopped."

"No, no that can't happen."

"It's happening as we speak."

"How many? Tell me how many dimensions he's destroyed!"

"His dark energy is sweeping across creation like a wave of destruction, corrupting and turning each realm into a twisted image of himself."

"What do you mean? I don't understand how this is happening, Tamara." She threw him through a thin rock face.

"You are in no position to demand anything. But I'll answer you because your questions amuse me. Luzige only needs a way into your reality. In my world, the energies are more subtle, and mere thoughts of separation and hatred aroused his awareness to us. He came swooping in not long after I enlisted your help."

"Yes, I found you through Auditum."

"You travelled into our dimension. We met once on a beach in our dreams."

"I remember."

"You were much stronger when I last saw you. You had become a being of pure light and energy. You maintained your appearance as you do now, for the most part, but you are only masking your true form."

"What do you mean? What true form?"

"You mean you don't remember? You don't remember any of this?"

"Remember what?"

"Who you are, James."

"No, I don't know who I am."

She laughed. "Perhaps that's why it's been so easy to topple you. You don't even remember your training. You have again forgotten the disciplines you once learned. The skills and lifetime of dedication to your craft." She sighed. "And that is exactly why Luzige is walking all over your dimension, just like all the others. How naive I was to think this time would be different. That you would be different."

"What do you mean, this time?"

"This is the seventh time you've ventured on this journey to stop Luzige. Prior to this, he has completely taken over your Earth reality six previous times. Now in this life time, he's attempting to destroy you once more. He's corrupting not only Earth you know, but also every variation of Earth in creation. There are multitudes of these variations, and he is seeing to it that all dimensions crumble beneath his feet. So far, he's succeeding. When we were last together, I thought we stood a chance. I thought there was a small hope of stopping him when I saw what you were capable of. But then he swallowed me up, like I was nothing, and pulled me back into this hellish world that used to be my home. I saw deep into him, James. Saw things that no one should see, saw that he's virtually unstoppable."

He was appalled at her words, which cut to the nerve of his very essence. There was something deep within him that he had failed to realize.

"Wait, what do you mean, virtually? That means you've seen a way to defeat him, haven't you?"

"What I've seen is the death and torment of innocent souls. I've seen the flesh ripped off bodies and pestilence and disease tear apart families and towns. I've seen him corrupt, torture, and destroy."

"No. You've seen something else. Tell me, please." She looked at him with a longing that he had not seen in a very long time.

"There was something I saw only once in his entire war on creation. Only one time did I see him ejected from a realm."

"What happened?"

"The host returned to its body."

"What do you mean?"

"The host. Luzige is a guest in the body of someone, which is his only means of physical access to our realms. And in this one case, the body's original soul found its way back. It made its way out of Luzige's hell world and found its way back to its body. Luzige had no choice but to leave."

"Why?"

"Those are the rules. If you can make it back to your body, the possessing demon has to leave. The bodies do belong to us, after all."

"So, that means I have to find Aidan's soul and return him to his body?"

"That's the only way I've seen him stopped."

He grabbed her shoulders. "Help me, Tamara. Help me stop him. You've changed. You've been corrupted by him, but there's still love in your eyes."

"We are all given a choice, James. And like Luzige, I've chosen to rule by fear."

"But that's the wrong choice. That's not who you are. I know you, Tamara; there's still love in you."

"Look at me. There is nothing left to love. He saw to that. He made me like this."

"No, Tamara, I-"

"Save it. You had your chance." She interrupted, looking around her surroundings in fear.

"The winds are changing. He's coming for you."

"Who?"

"Luzige. He knows you are here, and he wants to meet with you. He's stronger now. You are weak. He will crush you." All at once, the molten river slowed and became more burning embers and ash than flowing rock. The walls around the Caldron began to burn and crack. Ash began to collect on the ground and the air in the room became thicker, making it harder to breath. The denseness of the air turned bitter and a sense of fear trembled through the very ground James stood on. He looked at Tamara, still unable to grasp the implications of what would soon occur. She looked back at him, her flame-like eyes blistering in the darkness, her skin illuminated by a dark evil within. Her mouth opened for a single word of instruction.

"Run."

James collected what wits he had about him and started running towards the less-compromised part of the Caldron floor. He ran through the maze of pipes as the evil behind him chased him, thoroughly corrupting everything it came across. It was getting closer, moving in on his position as he did what he could to keep the momentum. He stopped to look back, only to see Tamara being overwhelmed and swallowed by the darkness. "Tamara!" He didn't stop for long, as the darkness took the form of a sandstorm of ashes, moving towards him at an incredible speed. Projectiles flew from the cloud as it devoured everything in its path, and Jacob was barely able to stay ahead of it. Running down the tunnel, Jacob tried to wake himself up.

James stumbled over himself as the dark storm approached. All he could feel was the white hot searing of his body as the cloud overtook him. A loud voice echoed throughout the storm, vibrating directly through James. "I CANNOT BE STOPPED." This was the last thing he heard.

He awoke with a jolt, covered in hot sweats. It was the middle of the night, and Joshua, Sarah, and Moretti were all sleeping soundly around him. He thought about what had just happened and quickly checked his body for any scars or wounds. He was fine, but still shook up.

"Hey, you. Are you all right?" Sarah sat up in her sleeping bag, looking at James.

"Yeah, I'm okay."

"How was your trip?"

"It was pretty scary, actually."

"Where did you go?"

"Another Earth, I think."

"Another Earth?"

"Auditum brought me to another dimension of Earth, the one Tamara's from. Luzige has corrupted her version of Earth, and he's in the same process of destroying our world right now."

"Can he be stopped? Can we do anything about it?"

"Yes, I think so."

"That's great news, right?"

"Yeah, except that Tamara's been captured and corrupted by Luzige. She's a different person now."

"No, don't say that. That's only his influence. I'm sure it's still her in there. What did she tell you?"

"Maybe you're right. She told me that when she merged with Luzige, she saw into his mind. There is a weakness we can exploit. I have to save Edward Aidan, that way the possession of his body will end, and Luzige will leave our realm."

"How are we going to do that? He's too powerful. He won't let you get to Aidan."

"I don't know, but we're going to try. There has to be a way. Even if I have to fight him in person and weaken him first, I will."

"No, James, he'll kill you. Like last time."

"I have to try, damn it. I've got to do something. I can't let him destroy all of creation. There's too much good and beauty that needs to be saved."

"Like what?" She stared at him with genuine curiosity. James looked deep into Sarah's eyes. She was very beautiful, especially in the light of the moon. He leaned forward slowly, and kissed her. He placed his hand on the side of her face, pulling her in. She grasped his shoulder, and moved closer towards him.

"Wait. I'm sorry, I shouldn't have done that."

"Neither should I, but it's okay. I think you're amazing, James. All the things you can do, your persistence, everything. It's brave."

"Thank you, Sarah. You're even braver than I am, and you've done so much already. Really, I mean it."

"Okay. Can we please stop this and get back to trying to stop the world from going to hell?" Joshua sat up, looking more than a little irritated.

"Yes," James said. "How much did you hear?"

"Too much. So now that you know you need to save Aidan, how do you plan on doing that? There's no way we can even physically get to him. He's either in some underground bunker or in one of his towers, locked away surrounded by his guards. Really big guards, I might add. No one has seen Luzige in months, only his generals."

"We have to find him. We have to force him out of Aidan's body. That's the only way to stop this madness."

"We're going to need some intel. We need to go see some people."

"Wouldn't his generals know where he is?"

"Probably, but there are seven of them, and each one of them would kill you about five times over before you could even ask them where he is." "Maybe." James grinned.

"Okay, so once we find him, then what?" Sarah asked.

"I have to first free Aidan from his prison, and then I have to confront Luzige."

"There's no way you can do this alone," Joshua said. "Luzige would be guarding Aidan with all of his might. How are you going to break through to free Aidan?"

"I don't know."

"I don't think we have much time. Luzige's dismantling of our world governments is almost complete. If he completely ruins our organized and civilized societies, masses will start reverting to survivalist tactics. We'll be ripe for the picking."

"How much time before Luzige's forces take over?"

"They've taken almost all of North America, and now he's spreading into Europe. I heard that the U.K. and Russia are mounting a united front, and they're trying to keep him out of the Middle East. It could be days, or weeks. There's no way to tell."

"I have to use the headset again. I'm going to go back for Tamara. I think I can convince her to help free Aidan. But you're right. I need some help." James looked towards Josh.

"Who are you going to enlist?" Josh asked.

"An old friend."

# TWENTY

## SEARCHING FOR PAUL

A FTER USING THE headset, he found himself walking along an old desert road. As he continued down the path, he thought of an old friend and teacher of his. The road was covered in sand, and the desert was large and barren. He approached a small encampment filled with people of Arab descent. He walked up to a man who was fixing his vendor stand for the morning as the sounds of a busy market came to life around him.

"Sir, excuse me. I'm looking for a young man. A teacher."

"Oh, you must be looking for Boulos."

"Yes, I knew him as Paul."

"Yes, yes, he is here. He lives in the city, farther up the way. He comes out from time to time to speak with seekers. They gather in front of him as he talks about the processes of life; he is helping prepare them for the transition. If you continue on, you might find him –Insha'Allah!"

"Thank you."

"You are welcome! If you like any of my art, please stop by." James nodded with a slight smile. He continued on, deeper into the city. This place was very bright in nature. James felt rejuvenated, and joyous in this place.

Seeing families playing in the streets, or couples having coffees at local shops reminded him of movies he had seen when he was living with George and Jessica up north. They'd watch some foreign films from time to time. George liked learning about other cultures.

James noticed artwork and jewelry, all of which seemed to have the same markings on them: a sun with pointed beams of light coming from the centre.

Turning a corner, he could see a large gathering of people sitting on pillows, listening to a man James could not see.

"And although we are at risk, our consciousness is eternal and will always live on in the creator. Even though our dimension is on the brink of destruction, all can be recreated in the eternal realms for all to enjoy. Just as we in the astral realms can enjoy these realities, so too will you enjoy the realms of the eternal."

"But teacher," a man asked, "why must we suffer this way and watch our astral worlds get destroyed like they are? Is this the will of the universe?"

"Suffering is a choice. The destruction of the universe is an eventuality, but as one universe dies, so too is another created. No, my friend, it is not the will of the universe that you suffer. Suffering is the will of the inhabitants of each dimension tormented by Luzige, for he cannot enter without invitation. By their choice do they allow destruction into their lives and realities, and likewise it is only by their choice that peace can be obtained."

"Is it not too late?"

"It is never too late, as time itself does not exist. There is only this moment, and in this moment we continue on and create peace within our minds and the minds of those around us. By doing this and by not entertaining the thoughts of fear, we will generate an even more powerful force, which can reverse the effects of Luzige." James moved in closer. There were about three hundred people sitting peacefully, listening to the man speak. He sat carefully and deliberately. His answers were soft yet confident. His words brought peace to the doubtful, and James could see why they admired him so much.

"Teacher!" An older soul raised his hand. "Why, then, are we subject to these forces?"

"Because in these dimensions, there exists an opposite for everything. There is a gradient range of experience, expression, and creation in any aspect of creation you can imagine. Light to dark. Hot to cold. Black to white. Love to Hate. This exists to provide a field of experiences and a range of possibilities to choose from, so each could have their own means to choose or work out their experiences of self. It is in this way that peace is found and creation of self is possible. You cannot create yourself if there are no options to choose from. What choice is the light, when there is only light?"

"So what is real and what is false?" Another wise student asked.

"Your choices are real. Love is real. All else is false and an illusion when speaking in eternal terms. The experiences of hate and fear may seem very real indeed, but they are not who you really are."

"So you're saying all experiences other than Love are the false options to choose from in the game of life?" James asked, standing up. "There is one answer, and it is Love. All else is there to distract you just enough to make the game interesting?" By now James realized the wise man was Paul, the one he was seeking.

Paul looked at him and grinned. He stood up. "Yes. That's exactly what I'm saying." He made a motion to his students and they picked up their pillows and stood up. They smiled and waved to Paul, looking curiously at James as they dispersed.

"Well, where's the fun in that?" James asked as they laughingly embraced each other.

"It's been a long time since I've seen you. How are you, my friend?"

"I'm doing fine, Paul; it's great to see you again. I'm sorry about what happened to you; you did not deserve that."

"It's okay; others have endured worse at his hands. I'm much happier since I left the earth realm anyway. There is so much more to explore in these worlds."

"Yes, but for how long? You know why I'm here, don't you?"

"Yes, of course. I've been expecting you. Our home world is in great danger; I know the prophecies of the Arabe'en are being fulfilled, one by one."

"I need your help. I think there's a way to stop Luzige and remove him from our Earth for good."

"What have you discovered?"

"That Edward Aidan must return to his body to stop Luzige. I also found Tamara. She was lost, but I found her."

"Yes, I heard she was taken by Luzige. I discovered this after my passing."

"I'm sorry about that; you were a great man and teacher to many. The Arabe'en missed you, and worked hard to carry on in your absence."

"Yes, I know they did. Unfortunately, they became overzealous and militant, losing most of the reason we were formed in the first place, as a source of peace and wisdom. I fear much of that was lost after I passed."

"You might be right. Many things have been lost. Much of North America has been taken over by his forces, and now he's entering Europe."

"Then there isn't much time."

"He hasn't taken everything, though. There's still time for Earth. I can stop all this."

"Tell me." Paul leaned in closer.

"I need your help to convince Tamara, and bring her back home. She's under a terrible spell, corrupted by his evil."

"That won't be easy."

"I know. Once we've freed her, we need to rescue Edward Aidan."

"What?" Paul paused for a moment. "Do you know what you're asking me to do? In all of creation, there is no worse place than where Aidan is this very moment. There is no greater place of pain and torment than that."

"Why is this world so powerful? How is this possible?"

"Because in all of creation, there is the expression of thought. All things were thought prior to becoming a thing. In these realms created by Luzige, he has envisioned a dampening field. You cannot even express thought properly, and you can't focus. You are so overwhelmed by fear and hatred that every horrible thing possible in your reality is shown to you. If you break, you are lost forever; there is no going back."

James shook his head in disbelief. "And Luzige has placed Aidan in this place?"

"Yes, in the deepest part of it."

"Then that's where I have to go, with or without your help. I have to try. I will not let Luzige have my world without a fight."

"You're not alone; I will go with you. As it was in the beginning, so it will be in the end. Together."

"Thank you, my friend."

"Come, there's much to be done. We can't go back into the depths without some magical protection." Paul went into his rather humble tent and came out with a small leather pouch. He reached in and took out a necklace. It was a familiar necklace, with a tear drop centre and diamond mount. James looked at it intently. It reminded him of the one he used to wear.

"Paul, is this the same necklace that I…"

"Well, to you, it is that necklace. What I have given you is a symbol of power. For you, it is a necklace. But when I hold it, it is a dagger. It takes the form of the beholder and becomes an enchanted object from your life, a symbol of strength, character and power. It is whatever it needs to be for you."

"What will it do?"

"It will act as a shield, and it will help you when you need it most. They say it was forged from the very tears of God. That's very poetic, but I'm not sure myself. It's extremely rare, no matter what dimension you're in."

"How did you get a hold of it?" He asked.

"Come now, James, you know I'm very resourceful, don't you?" Paul smiled.

"Of course, that's why I'm here."

"Good. Now, there is something else I need to give you." Paul turned around and grabbed a metal quarter staff from inside the tent.

"This is a very powerful tool and, similar to the necklace you now wear, will turn into any weapon you desire. It is manipulated by your thoughts. Here." He tossed it over to James and as he caught it, the staff instantly morphed into a short broadsword with a shimmering silver blade.

"Wow. Incredible."

"Indeed. You should also take these, they're arm guards. They will provide some shielding."

"Where are yours?"

"Don't worry, I have other weapons. All right, we need to move fast and get to Tamara before she's completely overwhelmed by his evil. Listen to me, where we're about to go, many before you have gone and lost themselves."

"What do you mean? I thought we just had to go back to where I found her."

"You mean, where she wanted you to find her. The Caldron was a trap; you were never supposed to leave that place. No. If we are to find Tamara, we must find her on her own terms. We must go where Luzige keeps all of his pets."

"Where's that?"

"It's the same place where he's keeping Aidan, I'm afraid. It's a sub-realm."

"What does that mean?"

"It's not really a fixed reality like you're used to. All of these realms have common elements, like the sky, the earth, gravity, or other dimensional attributes."

"Is that why I'm able to fly in some dimensions and not in others?"

"Exactly. Different realms have different properties. Such as cities, malls, landscapes, the sky. That's what you're used to, correct?"

"Yes, I suppose so."

"Now, *suppose* there were no common elements, and everyone in this reality created their *own* elements, their own ground, sky, or water.

What if everyone *was* their own reality? That's where we are going. There are no common elements, just a jumble of realities created by tormented individuals. It is the closest thing to Hell I've ever come across in my travels."

"Is there no return from this place?"

"You will return, but perhaps not as the same man as when you first arrived. This place will change you. What happens there is difficult to describe. I can only hint at it because it is simply another dimension entirely. What I can tell you is this: in some of the higher dimensions, the energies are so fast, so subtle, that the very fabric of reality can be felt. It is the feeling of creation itself, a sensation in the very air that you are loved, accepted, and a part of this unified field. But in the realm where we are going, there is no feeling of love. It is the very opposite of that: in the air there is a thickness, a heavy unsettling feeling of distrust, hate, and fear."

"A fear? Of what?"

"All fear you have come to know in your life will be used against you. There is no escape from yourself, your mind knows what you know, and you cannot lie to yourself. And in this world, you will be reminded of all of it. This has shattered the minds of many on earth, to even glimpse this place. Many of those walking the streets, those who are called insane, are simply those who have seen what this world has to offer and are forever changed."

"I see. So what is your guidance? How do we proceed?"

"You must realize the truth. Understand that even though you may have done things, said things, or thought things that may have been the most vile or evil during moments of your life, they pale in comparison to the many moments of joy you have brought to those around you. All of life has its reasons for interacting as it does. Whether in the form of sunny days or rainy, the gift is in the choice and the joy is in the balance. What you have done is nothing compared to what you are about to do, and that is to free reality itself from the tyranny of Luzige. We must band together and stop him from completely destroying our world before it's too late."

"Yes, you're right. This has to end; we can't let him destroy our dimension."

"Be resolute in that thought because it's time to go." Paul walked over to a black stone on his desk, paused for a moment and rubbed the stone with care. He stood before his bookcase as the shelves around him began to distort, and the wind rattled papers and books across the room. A large blue portal opened up directly behind him. "Let's go, James! Give me your hand!" James grasped Paul's hand as they flew through the door to another world. He felt the sensation of going through a wind tunnel, and flying through blue light. The light turned dark, and began bursting with red as they moved faster through the portal.

There were flashes of light as he recalled moments from his past life as Jacob. It started with the very earliest of his regret as a child: the unnecessary assault on another boy in class. James had smashed him over the head with both hands and had taken pleasure in it. The feeling of regret was amplified and made all the more vivid as he tumbled through the vortex.

Moments of his youth flashed next through his mind: taking joy in breaking toys, hurting animals for sport, and the shame of sexual exploration. He was being assaulted to his very core with his own choices and outcomes. The flying continued as he tried to focus on Paul who also looked like he was caught in a past memory. "Paul, snap out of it! Listen to me, we're just tumbling through this thing. Something's wrong!"

Paul continued to be locked in his own terror, as they both tumbled mercilessly through a never-ending portal of light and fire. Their velocity increased as did the flashes of light and bursts of memory. James saw himself walking through a doorway. It was a graduation party, and he saw himself dancing with a girl. A girl who was later badly beaten and raped by a group of boys at the party. James had done nothing. She cried out to him for help, but he was with some school friends and they had left her. It was a memory so locked away that it rocked James to his very core. He thought to himself how he was always leaving his responsibilities, always leaving when he was needed most. He felt ashamed that he had left that girl to suffer a horrific experience, that he had done nothing. A tremendous wave of doubt swept across him, weakening him even further.

Trying to escape the illusion, he called out once more. "Paul, listen to me, wake up!" Paul shook his head, and looked around at James.

"Try to get to me. Grab my hand!"

"What's going on, Paul?"

"Someone tampered with our portal; we need to find an exit!" Paul looked shaken and quickly fell back into trance.

"Paul, stay with me, are you okay?"

"Yes, come get me!" James flew towards him as best he could, finally grasping his arm.

"There, move towards the light!" They both leaned towards a shining light that became larger as they moved closer. They shot forward as they burst through, landing on a large dark plain of rocks. The world around them was a harsh, unwelcoming wasteland.

"We've made it through; we had to hold hands to ensure we'd both travel to the same location when we arrived here. Otherwise we'd both be in our own worlds, and trust me, that is not a good thing."

"So then where are we now?"

"I'm not sure, this could be landing zone. Some semi-common element belonging to this reality, perhaps created by the victims of this place."

"Or their jailors."

"Hmm, yes, good point."

"Who do you think tampered with our portal?"

"Perhaps it was Luzige trying to interfere with our plans."

"Good, that means we have him scared."

A familiar voice suddenly spoke to them. "You're pathetic. Do you actually think that Luzige would even bother with two insects like you? He has much better things to do, like torture your girlfriend."

"Lucious!" James stood up.

"Did you think you could get rid of me so easily? I live to serve him now. He asks me to follow you, so I follow you. He asks me to kill you, I kill you."

"It won't be so easy to fight both of us at once, Lucious."

Lucious laughed. "Take a look at your friend. It seems like he's having some difficulty confronting his past." Paul was toppled over to one knee and was mumbling something to himself.

"Paul, are you okay?" James moved in slowly to try and help as the mumbling got louder.

"I let them all die…"

"Paul, snap out of it. It's just a memory we have work to d—" Paul jumped up, his face enraged. His eyes had turned black and heat and embers sparked from him.

"I LET THEM ALL DIE!" Some form of acid was foaming from his mouth, and his eyes turned to flames likes Tamara's.

"I LET THEM ALL DIE AND YOU KILLED THEM!" Paul's fingers began to grow into sharp claws as he came slashing forward at James, who narrowly escaped his strike.

Lucious continued laughing. "You see, James, you have a very strong mind. Perhaps you can handle your own past sins. But for one like your friend who has led so many to suffer, he cannot withstand the torment of his own mind."

"You're a lunatic, Lucious!" James continued to avoid Paul's strikes, who was relentlessly venting his anger on him.

"He will not stop; he's enraged. He believes you killed his people. There were many Arabe'en slaughtered after Auditum was revealed to the world. They were implicated in using sonic sound to destroy cities all across the world. Every alcove of Arabe'en was snuffed out just like that. And because *you* were the source of Auditum, *you* killed them. And because he failed to kill you, he let them die! How ironic." Lucious's horrific laughed bellowed out of his serpentine belly and echoed across the wasteland.

"I cannot be held responsible for the actions of those acting out in revenge." James used minimal force in responding to Paul, in an effort to reason with him, dodging his slashes, tossing him off balance with ease. His claws and ravenous slashes grew stronger with each passing swipe.

"Those people did not deserve to die, but Luzige is at root cause of this because he destroyed those cities. Had those cities been saved, so too would the Arabe'en people have been saved. The actions of those murderers were not right, and shouldn't have happened, but Luzige still remains the root cause!" James shouted, trying to talk some sense into Paul and ignore Lucious's candour.

"That may be, James, but it's too late for your friend. His mind has been fractured, and there is no going back for him. He is gone…look at him!"

"No, that can't be! How do I snap him out of this?"

"There's no helping him, I said. It's over for him! You can try if you like, but don't waste your time."

"Lies!" Paul began growing larger and more ferocious, the evil surrounding them seeped into him like a poison.

"Believe whatever you want, it won't change his condition. The hate is festering inside him, the regret and fear is taking over. What's left of his soul is trapped in a spiral of never ending torment, just like the rest of the creatures in this forsaken place."

"Why are you telling me all this?"

"It amuses me to do so but might I make a suggestion?" Lucious got up off the boulder he was perched on, and crept behind it like a lizard.

"You might want to do something about your friend soon, before he gets out of hand. He's growing stronger by the second. He'll destroy us both at this rate."

"What would you have me do?"

"Send him to his maker. Take your weapon and end him before it's too late!" Paul grew husks, and shards of bone protruded through his skin as he grew larger and more massive each moment. Paul would pause and then crouch over slightly as dark energy seeped into him. He grew and stretched as it entered his body, muscles tearing, with his skin barely able to contain him.

"Why is this place turning him into a beast?"

"In this place dwells all the hatred and fear you could ever experience. And if you've done something you're not proud of, this place will draw it out of you and use it against you. It twists you and turns you into things like that: like your friend, like Tamara, and like me." Lucious motioned his boney finger towards Paul who was hunched over in pain. "You'd better do something about that; he's going to get worse."

"What do you want me to do?"

"You must let me back through the portal and give me the Blackstone he used to get here. That's the only way."

"What's so important about this stone?"

"It has properties; it's imbued with a type of dimensional warp, a vortex by which different energies can come through. With that, he can be restored."

"I don't trust you, Lucious; you've lied to me before, what's different this time?"

"As much as I may be distrustful, I do not wish to see you turned by these energies. Also, I must keep the stone after we are through, that's the deal."

"No way, I can't let you keep it."

"Ah, but you must. That stone is mine. And besides, you have no choice. You either give me the stone or you kill Paul, sending his consciousness into oblivion itself."

"Fine, go through the portal, but you'd better come back."

"I will, trust me." He gave a devilish grin, turning towards the vortex and jumped through.

James turned to a crouched Paul, who slowly was regaining his strength. He had increased in size significantly, with arms and legs the size of tree trunks. "Paul, you have to fight this. This isn't you."

"That's where you're wrong. There was too much evil in me, and seeing it all, feeling it all, I couldn't bare it. The hatred of this place seeped in like a poison, and now there's only Boulos left."

"Don't say that. You're not lost, you're just confused. It's this place that has done this to you."

"Is it? Is this place responsible for all my bad choices and failures? All of which led to our world being eaten alive by those locusts. No, those were all my doing, and yours." Paul stared at James, charging and flying at him with several strikes. His claws were deadly sharp, cutting James across the chest, sending him spiralling through the air.

Paul jumped up after him, grabbing him and throwing him to the earth, landing on top of him with vicious elbow drops. Turning aside, twisting James's leg, snapping it. The pain rocked James's body, but it healed quickly, given the properties of their dimension.

James struggled to his feet as Paul slammed into him from behind, sending him crashing into a pile of nearby rocks. James stood up, his face sliced from the impact, which again quickly healed. His body and clothes becoming soaked with blood, and he moved towards a nearby rock face for some protection.

"Paul, stop this, I'm your friend, please."

"Call me Boulos, Lukman. We are not friends." The rock face was lifted straight off the ground with tremendous force, and slammed back towards the earth on top of James. "I haven't been called that for a very long time, Paul."

"But that's who you are. You're the Lukman, the saviour. Who have you saved? Look around you, how many more dimensions must fall by your incompetence?"

"Listen to me, you have to stop this, it's Luzige, that's who we've come to stop! We can't separate now. Paul, please!"

Paul appeared from behind him with lightning speed. "My name is Boulos, Boulos!" Crashing his bare hands upon James's head, it sent him to the floor with a thunderous force. The portal opened once more with Lucious appearing from it.

"I've got the stone. I've got the stone!"

"Then use it, because I can't hold him off much longer." Lucious held the stone in the air. "James, remind him of himself, that's the only way to help restore him."

"Paul, listen to me. Whatever you think you've done, it was all part of the plan. You must accept the outcomes of your choices, whatever they were. If you aren't happy with what you've done, you've been given the chance to change and do better." The Blackstone in Lucious's hand began to glow.

"What you've done is not as important as what you will do. Focus on your new self, not the old. Let go, and release your hatred of yourself!" Paul listened to him and began to calm himself and change back to his original self. The Blackstone glowed even brighter as he returned to his natural state.

"Thank you, James. Thank you both," said Lucious.

"No need to thank me. That was business, fair and square."

"What do you mean business?" asked Paul.

"The Black Stone is his now."

"No, he can't have that!"

"A deal is a deal, old chum," laughed Lucious. "Would you rather be trapped down here like the rest of these fools?"

"A deal's a deal, and that's the only way I was able to free you. Let's focus on what's next; we need to find Tamara quickly."

"You don't know what you've done by giving him that stone. That stone could be used to trap Edward's soul, and thwart our chances of stopping Luzige." Paul sighed. "We'll get to Edward first. I need to find Tamara, she is most likely over the hillside over there. There seems to be a city a few kilometres away."

"Very good Paul, you're right. That's where he keeps them," said Lucious.

"Them?"

"Those he's going to sacrifice."

"All right, we've got to move fast," said James.

"Yes, well this is where we part ways. You two are on your own." Lucious began laughing and disappeared into the shadows.

# TWENTY-ONE

## LEFT BEHIND

THEY LOOKED AT where Lucious had disappeared. "That's not surprising. Since he turned, he's been more and more devilish as the day grows long." Paul said.

"That's fine; he can be whoever he wants. That's his choice, and in the end he'll have to face the consequences."

"Yes, just like us."

"How so?"

"Now that he has the Black Stone, it'll be much easier for him to travel to any dimension he chooses. And it's also going to make it harder for us to leave this place."

"Look, let's just get to Tamara."

"Over there, look." Paul pointed to a large staircase that went up several hundred feet, leading to a stone city. "That's where she is, James, in the city."

"Let's go." They quickly ventured up the stairs, moving at a brisk pace. They reached the top of the staircase, which lead them to a large stone door with lions and roses etched into the surface. There was a bell and pulley system to signal newcomers.

"Well, pull it," Paul said.

James grabbed the rope and pulled. The attached bell rung out loud and clear, opening the door slowly, revealing a light from within.

"Where are we, Paul?"

"I've never ventured this deep before; we're treading on new terrain here."

The door revealed a large corridor with doors and portals. James immediately sensed that each door led to another universe entirely. Each was another portal to a different dimension or a different parallel earth. They walked slowly and looked through each portal hoping to find Tamara. The portals were round and covered by a blue smoke. The dimensions themselves were instantly on the other side, so they continued to peer through and search for her.

James walked farther onwards, and got a strange feeling from one of the portals. He looked through and was grabbed by a large tentacle arm that tried to pull him through. Paul pulled him back, holding him steady. "Hold on!"

James pulled harder and released himself, but the creature continued to crawl out of the portal. It was half man and half giant squid. It had several arms, yet it had the feet of a large brutish man. It ran after Paul and James. They flew down the hall, breaking off into different directions.

"Go that way; I'll try to shake him off!"

"Okay! I'll meet you around the other side!" Paul shouted.

The rooms all seemed to connect, but they were all very different, some leading to infinity. He ran down the hallway, still trying to find Tamara but at the same time outrun this monster. He ran faster but as he did, he noticed his vision becoming 360 degrees in all directions. Allowing him to run forward, yet see the monster chasing him from behind. A useful tactic, as he was able to quickly shake him off, and lose him down a few corridors further into the city.

He stopped to get a sense of his surroundings. There were fewer doors now and even fewer portals. The stone seemed darker in these areas, less vibrant. The air was thicker, denser and wetter. He began to feel sickly, as if nausea was setting in. He put his hand up against a nearby wall, and looked over his shoulder as he gained composure. He thought Tamara might be caught up in a dream, so he checked it out. Going toward the bar, James could sense her presence. She was close by, and he was finally close to ending this mess.

Tamara was the only one who could track down Aidan and help end Luzige's reign of terror across their dimension before it was too late.

"James. You found me."

"Tamara? Is that you?" She looked stunning in a blood red dress, black lace, and deep red sword hanging from her side.

"Yes, it is."

"Do you know why I'm here?"

"Why, to rescue me of course."

"Yes, that's right. Now let's get out of here."

She laughed. "Silly boy. And what makes you think I need any saving?" She flew in the air, gripping her sword tightly, lashing out at James. He flew backwards, and she missed him by only a few centimetres.

"What are you doing?"

"It's time you realized something, James. You can't mess with other people's processes. If I want to stay evil, let me stay evil." She lunged forward, missing him by only a millimetres. She continued slashing at him, waving her hands and arms frantically.

He moved away with ease. His training and abilities seemed to effortlessly deal with the barrage of strikes.

"You've gotten stronger since we last fought, haven't you, James, or should I say Lukman?"

"I've learned a few things, yes."

"Good, then how do you plan on changing me back to your precious and innocent Tamara?

"I'll start by giving you this option: if you don't want to change back to the woman that I fell in love with, then don't. If you don't want to have a life with me and you'd rather live in this hell hole here, then go right ahead. I'm here for two reasons. The first was to figure out how I can stop Luzige, save Aidan and end all of this. The second was to free the woman I fell in love with. But you're not the woman I fell in love with anymore. Somehow that woman is gone and now I'm left with only one option."

"What's that?"

"To figure out how to save Aidan."

"I'll never tell you."

"I know." He began walking away.

"James, where are you going?"

"I'm leaving."

"So you're just leaving me here?"

"Yes." He continued on.

"How do you know I won't stab you in the back and kill you?"

"You won't. You can't, actually." Tamara stood there speechless, staring at James as he walked away from her. She loved him, and that part of her couldn't stand to see him go. Part of her walked away along with him.

"James, I still care for you." He stopped and turned towards her, looking directly into her eyes. With bright eyes staring back at him, she could see he loved her too. She walked towards him, and with each step, a piece of her dark armour fell to the ground, revealing her true form underneath. A bright and healthy beige flesh-toned skin revealed itself beneath a flowing white dress of pure white energy, her hair blonde as the sun, and eyes that burned with an intense brown. Tamara was back.

"It's you!" James ran to her, and they embraced with a deep and passionate kiss. They loved each other, and had longed for this moment for what seemed like an eternity.

"Thank you for coming for me."

"Paul came with me, but I haven't seen him. We parted ways in the tunnels."

"Those tunnels are very dangerous."

"Yes I can see that. Something chased me from one of the portals. It didn't find me though. I made it through and eventually got to you."

"We need to leave here, right now."

"Okay let's go. How do we—" Before he could finish, Tamara

grabbed his hands and they disappeared in a burst of light. They travelled through a swift and gentle portal of air, arriving in a beautiful grassy knoll. He couldn't discern their exact location, but it was gorgeous.

"Where are we?"

"We're back in the Summerlands, a place still untouched by Luzige," she said in a gentle voice.

"Good, we need to regroup. I think we should– ahh!" James gripped a wound by his stomach that suddenly appeared. A tremendous amount of blood began pouring out from underneath his clothes. He looked up at Tamara. "What's happening to me?"

"I don't know. Wait, your body, where is it?"

James buckled to the ground in pain. "Something's wrong, Tamara. Something's very wrong." Tamara closed her eyes.

"You're friends have been captured. They've taken the headset and left you behind."

"Who has? Who took them?" He writhed in pain. Tamara crouched beside him, trying to console him.

"I don't know. You have to get back to your body, James. You have to leave right now."

He returned to his body, which was left in the middle of the forest. His body was stripped of any valuables, and he was left for dead. He had a gaping stomach wound, probably from a knife. He rose to his feet, blood pouring out of him.

There was no sign of Joshua, Moretti, or Sarah. The night was dark and cold. James was beginning to freeze, with his blood being the only source of heat he could feel. He did his best to put pressure on the wound and looked around but saw absolutely nothing. He must have been in an Auditum-induced blackout when their camp was raided. *They took everyone as prisoners, and they must have thought stabbing and leaving me for dead would finish me off.* They were probably right.

To Be Continued…